ASHLEY BUNDY

Dreams of Darkness

Beyond Blackwood Manor: Book One

First published by Ashley Bundy 2025

Copyright © 2025 by Ashley Bundy

All rights reserved. No part of this publication may be reproduced, stored or transmitted in any form or by any means, electronic, mechanical, photocopying, recording, scanning, or otherwise without written permission from the publisher. It is illegal to copy this book, post it to a website, or distribute it by any other means without permission.

This novel is entirely a work of fiction. The names, characters and incidents portrayed in it are the work of the author's imagination. Any resemblance to actual persons, living or dead, events or localities is entirely coincidental.

Ashley Bundy asserts the moral right to be identified as the author of this work.

First edition

This book was professionally typeset on Reedsy.
Find out more at reedsy.com

*To everyone who
ever survived a haunted house.*

Acknowledgments

What can I say, bookworms? This book was a merry little adventure. An adventure I might not have taken if it hadn't been for all the fans of the duology asking me what happened after. Plus, let's face it, Margaret deserved a chance to tell her story. With that being said, I have to start off the acknowledgements with all of the fans! You have no idea what your dedication means.

Now on to my beta readers Nancie Blume, Callie Pey, Kat Bethel, and Jen Cooper. You ladies have all given me a unique perspective that helped shape this book into the best possible version of itself. Thanks to each of you. I love you bunches.

My editor, Jenny Sliger of Owl Eyes Proofs and Edits, is the absolute best. Thanks for the detailed feedback and quick turnaround times. You keep my little overly stressed heart on task, and that's a feat that can't possibly be explained.

On a personal front I'd like to thank my boyfriend, Don for his unyielding patience with my sometimes hectic deadlines.

Let's get into a technical confession. I almost had to push this project back by a lot, but a generous contribution from someone who wishes to remain anonymous made it possible for me to stay on schedule. You know who you are, and thank you from the bottom of my overly stressed heart. You have no idea what this means to me.

Lastly, I'd like to thank Wendy Sizemore, Graceli Kaye, and

Megan Russ. You are the cheerleaders that keep me going. I love you all.

CHAPTER ONE

Remi-2022

The nightmares started when Remi was pregnant with her second child. She hadn't said anything to her husband, Richard, because she didn't want to alarm him.

She'd heard that dreams weren't uncommon in pregnant women, and she hadn't thought much of it at first. Until she started having visions of babies roasting in fires and the face of a young girl with large eyes, staring at her from a dark corner of the cellar.

These things rang alarm bells in her mind, but she chose to ignore them. The history of Blackwood Manor, the plantation home she resided in with her husband, had a terrible history for several generations. Richard inherited the land three years before, and they'd done a deep dive into the home's history, banishing the darkness that plagued the land once and for all. Or so they'd thought. Nothing happened in the three years since. The land flourished, and they'd slowly begun to soothe the fears of everyone in town. They now ran a successful bed & breakfast in Blackwood Manor.

Remi continuously dismissed her nightmares throughout her pregnancy. She did her best to find any logical explanation she could. She was overtired, her hormones were going crazy, she was thinking of the bloodshed that once cursed the land. It was easy enough to do, and she was convinced they would stop after she gave birth. They didn't.

"Don't you ever sleep, Remi?"

At two o'clock in the morning, she hadn't expected to see anyone in the kitchen after entering from the back staircase. She cinched her robe tighter and nodded at Gus.

He was seated at the kitchen island eating a bowl of cereal, and he grinned at her when she entered.

"Who's out front?" she asked him, going for the coffee pot.

"Natalie dropped in." He narrowed his eyes at her. "Seriously, coffee? You need sleep."

She shook her head. "Can't afford to right now. Midterms start Monday." It was a handy excuse even though it was an outright lie. She was prepared for midterms, and she'd been finished with her work for a week.

"Kylie sleeping through the night yet?"

Remi laughed and grinned at him slyly.

"She's five weeks old."

Gus's expression didn't change as he stared at her. Remi sighed. "No. She's not sleeping through the night. But she's doing well for her age. It's honestly Emily I'm worried about."

She bit her lip as she remembered the meltdown her older daughter had at bedtime the night before. Emily was always a good sleeper, down without argument, and sleeping through the night until the week Kylie was born. She started resisting, asking for extra bedtime stories, and suddenly needing to pee every hour, but last night was the worst of all. She'd screamed at the top of her lungs and thrashed in her bed so hard Richard was forced to take her to the cottage out back for the night. They were worried the guests would think they were torturing her.

"Ahh, don't worry about it. Terrible twos are a thing."

"I know. It's that she was different last night. Something about it scared me."

"What about it?"

"She kept saying the girl was being mean to her."

Gus sat back for a moment and gave her a thoughtful look before speaking again. "Do you think—"

"I think being here, we'll always question these things," she shrugged. "But nothing has happened for three years. You've seen the change in this place. Natalie's here all the time. Surely, she'd know if anything was still here. Kids do have imaginary friends."

"But it makes you uneasy."

She nodded. "It does."

The baby monitor in the pocket of her robe went off and Kylie's soft cry broke an uncomfortable silence. "Well," she smiled at Gus. "Duty calls."

"Remi?" he said as she turned toward the staircase.

"Yeah?"

"Don't worry. I'm sure it's a phase."

Remi nodded and made her way up the stairs. She was lost in thought.

Emily had turned into another child entirely. Everyone kept telling her not to worry, you can't escape the terrible twos. This behavior seemed so abrupt and excessive. It didn't feel normal.

It was times like these that Remi wished she could talk to

her family and get guidance, but that wasn't an option.

She had a privileged upbringing compared to her husband and friends, but that didn't mean she hadn't had obstacles of her own to overcome. It was nearly impossible to explain to them she admired their freedom because she'd grown up with her every thought being dictated. The moment she'd grown a spine and started pushing back, she'd become the black sheep of the family. She had no more of a relationship with her family now than the others did.

Remi stepped through the doorway to the family wing and made her way to the nursery. She stared down at her baby daughter, Kylie. She was sleeping soundly. Remi furrowed her eyebrows and pulled the baby monitor out of her pocket. She knew she'd heard Kylie crying. Gus heard it too, hadn't he?

She knew she should be grateful Kylie fell back to sleep so quickly, but she couldn't help feeling a bit of unease. That, with Emily's bizarre behavior, set her nerves on edge. Something about the whole thing felt unnatural.

Remi grabbed a blanket off the window seat and settled into the rocking chair in the corner.

If anyone could see her right now, they would think she was overreacting. She'd been accused of it in the past. But this sense of dread was worse than it had been in the past three years. The last time she'd felt this way was when the group were preparing for the final battle. There had been intense relief in her gut the moment it was all over, and she'd simply known the property was cleansed.

Ever since childhood, she'd been able to sense things. She'd never tried to talk to anyone about it though. How could you explain something you didn't understand? She wasn't like Natalie. Natalie's gift was self-explanatory. If she touched things she could get visions of things that happened in the past or hear a person's memory. It wasn't like that for Remi.

Remi knew what people were feeling. She would often absorb those feelings and experience them herself, but she couldn't see things that occurred or know the why behind various tragedies. It was torture.

When she'd first set foot inside Blackwood Manor, she'd known something wasn't right. It scared her. She'd experienced this so often it was second nature, but she'd never felt that way with a place before. Richard told them all the stories of his childhood. She knew all about the history of the property, the supposed hauntings driving people out in droves, but she hadn't really believed it.

Her gut feeling was rarely off, and now it was doing a theatrical production. Something was wrong. That was obvious.

Now, sitting in the nursery, it was hard for Remi to believe how far they'd come. The journey to the here and now had been a long one. It was dangerous and toxic at times.

Remi's eyebrows knit together as she thought about how their little group was two people short following that battle. She missed them fiercely. The battle was done. They'd won. The time to leave would have been before, but Remi would never expect someone she cared about to stay in a place that caused them so much pain.

They'd all dealt with the tragedy of loss during the final battle. It took time to deal with that. The peace that overcame the property when they'd won was almost instantaneous but that didn't mean that scars healed the same way.

Over the course of the past several weeks, Remi felt the peace slowly melting away. She'd tried to talk to Richard about her fears, but he hadn't taken them seriously.

"You're tired from being in medical school, having a baby, and chasing after a toddler. You need more sleep, babe," he'd told her. She'd never brought it up again.

Remi wasn't some meek woman who was afraid of her own shadow, despite what some may think upon first meeting her. She was, however, one to pick her battles. Life was too short to spend it fighting over the little things. So, she kept her mouth shut. After all, Richard wasn't being intentionally dismissive. She was the one who couldn't seem to figure out how to explain what she was sensing.

Having nightmares? It didn't automatically mean anything. Baby crying on the monitor, but the baby is asleep when she comes in the room? Anyone would think the baby simply fell asleep. There were logical explanations for everything. But that sick, twisted knife in Remi's gut told her there was more bubbling under the surface. Was the house waking up? Was it even possible?

CHAPTER TWO

Margaret-1862

"It's a girl." Josie held up the tiny baby at long last. The labor was hard and daunting, far worse than the births of her first two babies. The pain had been everywhere all at once, and Margaret thought it would never end.

She felt like she was being split in half. The pain radiated throughout every part of her body. Her legs continued to shake, and her lungs burned with every taxing breath she took. She wouldn't be at all surprised if Josie told her the most intimate part of her had been ripped to non-existence. The pain there was so brutal she almost couldn't feel it anymore. But the warm stickiness of the blood on her thighs served as a reminder.

Josie detected something was wrong early on.

"I can't see the head," she said.

"Can you see anything?" Margaret cried. How could she not see the head? It made no sense. The damn thing was right *there*, the pressure cruel and unyielding.

"I think it's upside down."

Josie wanted to go for a doctor in town, but Margaret

wouldn't let her. Then her shame would be known. She'd carefully hidden her pregnancy, and she couldn't throw that away now. Besides, it was a good thing. The baby being upside down was God's way of protecting her shame. Maybe it would get stuck and die!

Eventually, when her screams became too loud and frequent, Josie shoved her hand inside her to turn the baby. Margaret saw white at first, fearing she would pass out, then felt the give and release as the baby slipped from her body.

She instinctively turned to see the baby in Josie's arms but could bear it for only a few seconds before averting her gaze.

Why hadn't it died? She squeezed her eyes tightly shut and sent up a silent prayer for the shame of having such a thought. She'd be lying to herself and anyone else though, if she hadn't wished for it.

When the labor began showing signs of difficulty, her heart soared. She'd believed her answers were being answered. That God was taking away this cross, so she needn't bear it. But the child had been born.

Why? Why had this happened to her? She was a good, Christian lady. She'd always tried to put others above herself and do right by anyone she knew.

She'd made one mistake, had one moment of weakness. Riddled by loneliness, she'd turned to Josie for comfort. Oh, she'd known it was wrong. Her John was a wonderful husband and father, and he hadn't deserved her betrayal. She regretted the act instantly.

Almost immediately after they'd finished, they'd heard the horses of the approaching Union soldiers who forced their way in and set up camp in the house for months.

The men didn't merely sleep in the spare bedrooms. Oh,

CHAPTER TWO

no. They committed vile acts on both Margaret and Josie, stole food and anything else of value, and destroyed prized possessions before riding away into the night. It wasn't long before Margaret began to suspect she was with child.

She knew if this was her punishment for betraying her husband, she should accept it. She hadn't fought when the men came into her room at night. She felt like she deserved it.

But the child? That was too much. She'd taken her punishment without argument and now she would have to endure this? How long would she have to pay for one mistake?

Yes, she'd prayed the child would die in her womb, and long before the birth complications. She did feel guilty for it. After all, it wasn't the child's fault she'd been unfaithful to her husband. All she'd done was be born. Margaret knew that. But she couldn't control the feelings of shame.

How was she supposed to explain this child? Everyone knew when John went to fight in the war and the timeline didn't line up. She wouldn't be able to convince anyone this was her husband's child.

"Would you like to hold her, Miss Margaret?" Josie asked from the corner where she was washing the baby off from the basin.

Margaret shook her head violently. "No. No, thank you, Josie. Maybe later."

"Alright, well if you don't feel well enough to nurse her right now, I'll go down and make a bottle for her." Josie raised an eyebrow, as if questioning if this was what she really wanted. Of course she was.

If Margaret wouldn't feed this child, they'd have no choice but to use a mixture of milk and animal broth. That could be extremely risky for babies and should only be used in the most deplorable situations, but she wasn't ready.

Josie sighed, wrapped the baby in a blanket, and lowered her into the bassinet. "Do you need me to help you get cleaned up before I go?"

"No, that's alright. Bring me the basin, please."

Josie carried the wash basin and a clean cloth to Margaret's bedside table before exiting.

Margaret sat up in the bed slowly, her limbs and uterus screaming in protest at the abuse and began to wash off.

The baby cried. Margaret sighed as her heart swelled, and her breasts began to ache with the need to nurse. She'd been convinced that not nursing this child would be easy, since she didn't have the same emotional bond that she had with Lucy and Percy, but there was milk seeping out of her nipples. Why was her body betraying her? Did it not know that everything this child stood for would be her downfall?

She shakily got to her feet and walked to the bassinet, unbuttoning the front of her nightgown as she went.

The baby's face was scrunched up and beet red, with its eyes tightly squeezed shut when Margaret peered down at her. She swung her tiny fists as though trying to break free from something horrendous. Margaret smiled before she could think. She'd felt many times throughout the pregnancy that she was being beaten. It wouldn't surprise her if her insides were black and blue. It was no wonder if the child did this inside the womb as well.

Margaret was reaching down to pick the baby up when she opened her eyes. Margaret stumbled back, her eyes going wide with horror. Her newborn baby's eyes were black. Her suspicions were confirmed. There was a demon inside her baby.

CHAPTER THREE

Remi

"Remi? Remi? Baby, you okay?"

Remi snapped her eyes open, and her heart gave a little jolt. She stood over Kylie's crib, gripping the railing tightly.

She stared down at her baby, who slept soundly. She wasn't swinging her fists as if wildly trying to escape, and she didn't stare up at Remi with eyes that were blacker than night. So why had she thought so?

Remi was completely unnerved, not knowing where the thoughts came from or how she got from the rocking chair to the crib. She jumped when a hand gripped her shoulder.

"Relax, baby. It's me."

Remi looked up and unclenched at the sight of her husband standing beside her.

"Richard?"

His brows narrowed with concern, and he gently rubbed her back in small, circular motions. "Are you okay?"

"I'm fine." She gave him a tight smile, but his eyes remained narrowed. "I thought I heard her crying. "

Richard peered down into the crib and back at her. She knew

what he was thinking because she was thinking it herself. She was going crazy. Neither of them would say so out loud, but it was there under the surface.

"Come on," Richard said finally, gently tugging on her arm to pull her from the room. "Let her sleep."

CHAPTER FOUR

Remi

Remi regulated her breathing by the time Richard led her down the back staircase into the kitchen, but the worry was still on her mind.

Emily sat in her highchair at the end of the island with their friend Natalie making silly faces and spoon feeding her mushed up oatmeal.

Natalie was instrumental in the battle three years ago. Richard contacted her because he'd been told she was psychic, something he'd figured could be instrumental in the investigation, and it was. Natalie's ability to see things through touching a person or object was spectacular. She'd given them answers to so many things they hadn't even known were questions.

Natalie glanced up from her place at the island, and her expression instantly went serious.

Don't let her get too close, Remi thought to herself. *Don't let her touch you.*

Remi knew she was being irrational. Natalie could give her some insight into what was wrong, but that was exactly why she didn't want to be touched. She was afraid to know what was going on. The less she knew, the better off she was.

"What's wrong?" Natalie asked.

"Nothing. Just tired." Remi plastered a smile on and made her way to the coffee maker to pour herself a cup.

Natalie flicked her eyes to Richard. "You gonna tell me the same thing?"

"I found her standing over Kylie's crib with a vacant expression on her face. I said her name four times before she responded to me."

Snitch! Remi couldn't believe her husband ratted her out. Richard should know her well enough to understand if she was keeping something to herself there was a reason.

Natalie's eyes snapped back to her, and she rose to her feet. "Why are you lying to me? What's going on?"

"Nothing, really. I had a rough night. I mean with somebody's temper tantrums. I had a sleepwalking moment." Remi's eyes flipped to Emily in her highchair, munching away and appearing annoyingly well rested.

Natalie raised her eyebrow and smirked. "Sleepwalking?"

"Yeah. I went through a sleepwalking stage in high school. All the pressure of the college prep classes. I guess it's back."

Great. Now she was blatantly lying. She'd never sleep walked once in her entire life. Worse, she hadn't even thought about the lie. It tumbled out of her mouth so easily; it was as if she had no control over it.

Natalie gave her a final glance before turning her attention back to Emily. Richard, however, didn't take his eyes off her. The lie may have been enough to pacify Natalie, but she could never fool Richard. He knew her better than she knew herself. Thankfully he didn't say anything, but she knew they'd be talking about it tonight.

CHAPTER FOUR

"Well," Remi sat her coffee cup in the sink, "I'm going to go grab a shower and head out. I have an early class."

Another lie. Richard knew her class schedule, but he didn't call her on it.

Remi didn't feel nearly as silly for this lie. She needed time alone to calm her nerves and process what happened. Richard would understand that. He'd always been good in that way. He knew when to push her and when to hold back. He wore the ability to interpret her needs like a second skin and she was thankful to have a husband who was so in tune with her.

As she stepped into the shower, she allowed herself to think back on the dream. She remembered this one vividly, when she hadn't fully remembered all the others in the morning. It shocked her to realize this was more like a memory than a dream.

She was Margaret Blackwood, moments after giving birth to Gloria, and she'd experienced a plethora of emotions in rapid succession. Pain, disappointment, shame, and the uncontrollable need to comfort her baby despite it all.

Was this really how the day of Gloria's birth had unfolded? Margaret and Gloria were two spirits Remi never encountered. Their spirits left the manor the day Richard's family died. She'd heard enough about them, though, to have very strong opinions on the whole history.

Margaret Blackwood had been a loving woman who turned dark and cruel, locking her youngest child in the cellar as soon as she was old enough to walk.

It was the easiest way for the woman to ignore the child's existence, and most people that Remi talked to on the matter thought Margaret was a heartless witch because of it. Remi felt the same way when she'd first heard the story, but the more she learned, the more Remi couldn't help but feel sympathy for the woman.

That was a different time, and for her to bear a child that was not her husband's, even if it was from an attack beyond her control, would be a source of great shame.

Plus, they'd found letters indicating Margaret grieved her actions. Remi didn't think Margaret was heartless. She thought the woman was in an impossible situation she didn't know how to come back from and lost her mind. Maybe she'd even experienced untreated postpartum depression. Remi felt bad for the child, of course. Poor, sweet Gloria deserved better. It was a horrible situation all the way around. There were no winners or losers in that situation.

She'd tried to explain her thoughts on the matter once, and her friends tore her a new one. At the time, she didn't know why they'd taken such offense to her saying she didn't think Margaret was *all* bad. It dawned on her later that they all had crappy home lives as children, and it clicked for her. They couldn't sympathize with Margaret because they saw themselves in Gloria.

As sorry as she was for Margaret, she didn't want to be inside her head. Having those thoughts, and that wave of emotions, made her extremely uncomfortable. It was more than simply observing through a lens. She'd felt like she *was* Margaret, and these awful thoughts were about her own baby.

She loved Kylie, and Emily too. Her eldest's difficult bedtime routine was making her crazy, but she couldn't shake the thing she'd said during last night's meltdown. *"The girl is mean."*

A chill ran down her spine the moment it was said. Was this girl the reason her daughter was behaving so erratically suddenly? Who was the girl? What was she doing to Emily?

CHAPTER FOUR

If Richard was startled by it, he hadn't said anything. He'd only focused on trying to soothe Emily before finally choosing to take her out to the cottage.

It was somewhat of a relief that Gus asked the same question that was on her mind when she'd told him about it. "Do you think?"

In another location, the temper tantrums of a two-year-old might not get a second thought, especially when it came to bedtime, but Blackwood Manor was no ordinary location. Ghosts prowled the halls and the grounds for centuries, including one vindictive little blonde girl. Was it Lucy tormenting her daughter? If it was, what did it mean?

Remi turned off the water and got out of the tub, straining her ears for any noise out of the ordinary as she toweled off. All she heard were the sounds of bed & breakfast life that had become common place.

When she went downstairs, she took the front stairwell. It was within regular business hours now, and she was fully dressed. She only used the back staircase for quick trips in the middle of the night when she was in her pajamas. The narrow, creaky stairs creeped her out.

Her bad mood was temporarily lifted when she glanced into the dining room to see all the tables filled. It was a miracle they'd been able to build a business in Blackwood Manor when people refused to come near it for the longest time.

Remi smiled at Jessie, who was waiting tables, and she smiled back at her. She jumped when a hand clasped over her shoulder.

"Gotcha," Natalie hissed in her ear before whirling her around.

Damn it. Why did Natalie always have to be so sneaky?

Natalie narrowed her eyes and tugged her into the parlor before crossing her arms in front of her and glaring at Remi.

Remi shot her gaze at the floor and tried to think of a good enough lie.

"What? Speak." Natalie snapped.

Remi cleared her throat and stared back up into her friend's eyes. She might be able to appease someone else on the matter, but there was no sense trying to bullshit Natalie.

"What do you want to know?"

"How many times have you had the dream?"

"I don't know."

Natalie tightened her lips.

"Really," Remi insisted. "I've been having nightmares since I was pregnant with Kylie, but I've never been able to remember them in the morning. At least not the entirety. I'll remember bits and pieces. Like a movie that plays when you walk in and out of the room. This was the first time I remembered the whole thing. I think it's because Richard interrupted me."

Natalie's eyes softened, but her tone remained hard. "You didn't think you should tell someone this?"

"No. It's not uncommon to have strange dreams during pregnancy, and I couldn't remember them anyway. It didn't seem important."

"Alright, but if it happens again, I want to know about it."

Remi nodded. "I can agree to that. I wanted to ask you—you were with Emily this morning; did you pick up on anything new or different?"

Natalie's eyes widened "No. Why?"

"Nothing. It's probably nothing."

"Remi."

Remi sighed. "Her tantrums at night have been worrying

me. Then last night she said a girl was being mean to her. I thought maybe—"

"I don't know," Natalie said finally. "We'll all sit down tonight and see if we can figure out what's going on. Compare notes and all that jazz. For now, I'll let you get to *school*." She dragged out the last word with emphasis and cocked an eyebrow.

Remi felt immense relief. Natalie knew she didn't have class, but she was giving her an out. Her friend knew she needed time to de-escalate. Natalie was good like that.

Remi hugged Natalie goodbye and walked out the front door, making her way to her car.

CHAPTER FIVE

Remi

Remi found herself at a table in a quaint little coffee shop in town. She waved when she saw her friend, Sophia, walk in and rubbed her coffee cup for warmth.

Sophia made her way over chuckled at the sight of the coffee cup in her hands. "I swear, Remi, if you don't watch out, you're going to turn into a cup of coffee."

The laughter left her face as quickly as it appeared. Remi didn't have a good poker face with anyone, but she was especially vulnerable with Sophia.

"What's wrong? Are you okay?"

Remi told her everything in a hushed tone as the barista brought over another coffee for Sophia. She didn't feel the same hesitation about telling Sophia things as she did most of her other friends. There were a few different factors behind that. One, Sophia didn't have a history with Blackwood Manor and therefore wasn't biased. She had, of course, been to visit, but it was after peace times, and she knew nothing of the horror that used to plague the place. Two, while her childhood hadn't been sunshine and roses, she didn't have the fractured upbringing the others did, like Remi, and could be more objective in certain situations.

"Wow," Sophia sat back in her chair and ran her fingers through her silky brown hair.

"What do you think?" Remi asked tentatively. She needed somebody to tell her what to do.

"I don't know, chick." Sophia shook her head. "It's hard to know what to think. You're the mama bear. What is your gut telling you?"

Remi took a moment to consider, then carefully chose her words. "I don't want to jump to conclusions, but my gut is telling me something isn't right."

"Then there's your answer."

"The only thing that's giving me doubt is the fact that nothing has happened while I'm awake."

"Except your daughter screaming bloody murder and talking about someone being mean to her."

Remi bit her lip. "Yeah," she whispered.

Sophia squeezed her hand. "Hey. It could all be a coincidence. Maybe it's the stress of midterms. I say, as long as it's dreams, let it go. But be cautious. I want you to pay close attention to your surroundings and Emily's behavior. And the moment anything crosses over from being dreams into reality, that's when you run."

Remi nodded and took a long swig from her coffee.

* * *

The get-together lifted Remi's spirits. She felt better about the whole situation and went home with her head held high.

When she got home, Remi walked around the side of the house to enter through the door to the kitchen. She didn't want to use the front entrance and deal with customers.

Meow!!

Remi jumped as a shadow flew through the air, landing next to her on the island. She lifted a hand to her chest and stared down at the offending cause.

Their cat, Whiskers, sat on the island and began grooming her coat.

"Whiskers! You about gave me a heart attack!"

The cat stared up at her with lazy eyes before continuing to groom herself.

"Get off the counter," Remi said. She picked Whiskers up, who hissed, and carried her to the servant's stairwell.

They allowed the cat to roam the house at will, and for the most part, customers loved it. If there was an allergy, they'd deep clean that customer's room prior to their arrival and keep Whiskers in the family wing during their stay. The rest of the time, though, she was free to roam. Except for the kitchen and dining room. They never allowed her where food was prepared for health code reasons. Remi grabbed cleaners from under the sink and began to scrub down the island where the cat sat. She'd have to remember to talk about making sure those doors were tightly secure at the meeting that night.

"Hey, babe." Richard entered from the staircase and wrapped his arms around her waist before planting a kiss on her forehead.

"Hey. Where are the kids?"

"Out for the count," he said suggestively and leaned in to

CHAPTER FIVE

place a kiss on her lips, but she leaned back.

Had she heard him right? "You're letting her sleep?"

He seemed shocked by the question. "Well, yeah. She's two years old. She needs sleep, Remi."

"If she sleeps all day, she won't sleep at night. This is why we're having problems with her."

He stepped back as if she'd slapped him. Remi sighed. She hadn't meant to snap at him, but damn it, where was the common sense?

"It's normal for kids to take naps."

"Not when they're up all night. Honestly, I'm exhausted here. Between her tantrums, the baby, and school, I'm running on fumes."

"I seem to recall that *I* was the one who was up all night with her," Richard growled.

"Wow." Remi tossed her sponge at his chest and ripped the gloves off her hands. "You can make lunch for the guests. And stop letting Whiskers in here if you don't want to get shut down."

Without waiting for a reply, she made her way up the servant's staircase. It was time for a nap of her own.

CHAPTER SIX

Margaret-1863

Margaret's life became a fog. She was a person she didn't recognize and didn't like very much, but she was unable to control the sharp sting of words aimed at everyone around her.

With each passing day, the heaviness in her chest grew. There was a constant ache in her shoulders from tension, and any noise made her want to snap.

This was especially difficult with children in the house, particularly an infant. Percy was a quiet child, even when playing outside, and was mindful of his studies. His nose was always buried in a book when he was indoors. He was the easy one.

Lucy, her princess, was more childlike but easily corrected. If she made noise, all it took was a gentle reminder and a hug to quiet her down. It helped that Lucy was the loving one, giving her kisses, offering to rub her feet, and bringing her drawings nearly every day. It was Lucy that kept her sane through it all.

Then there was the other one. The youngest. She irked

CHAPTER SIX

Margaret. Josie thought Margaret didn't even try with the girl, but she was wrong. Margaret did try with every breath of her body not to hate the small child. The circumstances of her birth were hard enough, but she was a difficult child in general. She never stopped crying. The wailing would go on for hours, despite their best attempts at soothing her.

The girl would scream until her face was blood red, kick her legs violently, and even hit herself. Bruises were a regular occurrence.

Dealing with her was so exhausting. It seemed every time Margaret finally began to drift into sleep, the sharp, piercing screams would cut through the night, bouncing off the walls, and awaken everyone.

Josie said they needed to be patient with her, but Josie didn't have to live in the house with her. She was able to retire to the servant's quarters at night and have uninterrupted sleep. It was wildly unfair.

When the girl retired from her bassinet, she'd tried putting her in a room with Lucy. This was mainly at her daughter's request. She'd bounced with excitement, talking about how she couldn't wait to play dollies with her baby sister.

Margaret always felt a flash of anger at those words, but she pushed them down for Lucy's sake. She hated hearing the girl referred to as sister, daughter, anything to remind her they were related. Biologically, it might have been so, but that thing was not her daughter.

Finally, one night, after four consecutive days of no sleep, Margaret snapped. She'd cried herself to sleep and was only under for five minutes when the wailing began again.

She'd shot from her bed and into the girl's bedroom, snatched the covers back, and grabbed the squealing girl.

"Mama? Mama, what's wrong?" Lucy asked.

Margaret ignored her and hauled the girl down to the cellar and deposited her roughly in a corner.

She felt guilt momentarily as the girl's big, frightened eyes stared up at her, but she'd forced herself not to be taken in by it. The only thing that worked in these matters was discipline.

"If you're going to scream, you can sleep down here!" she snapped. "Scream away!"

She'd marched straight back upstairs and finally gotten a full night's rest.

The following morning when Josie came in to make breakfast she'd stuck her head in the bedroom. "Miss Margaret?" she'd asked. "I've just gone to wake the children. Where is the little girl?"

"She's in the cellar."

Surprise filled Josie's face. "The cellar, ma'am?"

"She wouldn't stop screaming."

The surprise turned into horror. Margaret was filled with rage seeing the horror on Josie's face. Honestly, what was she supposed to do?

"Oh, don't look at me like that," she'd hissed. "I needed one night's sleep. You don't know what she's like."

That night turned into a downward spiral. Internally Margaret could admit that, but she would never voice wrongdoing out loud. Because sleep had been so peaceful that night, Margaret decided that the girl's bedroom should permanently be the cellar. Josie didn't argue with her when she moved blankets and pillows down, but she shot her the most hateful sneer.

It was for the good of everyone! Margaret didn't know why that was so difficult to understand. She wasn't trying to be malicious. The other children were growing and needed adequate sleep to thrive. How was she supposed to be able to mother the children and run the plantation when she wasn't sleeping? It was even in the girl's best interest. In the dark with no distractions, sure she would cry a bit, but she'd fall asleep faster when her antics weren't getting attention.

But Josie now saw her as a monster. This sweet girl, who she'd watched blossom into a beautiful young woman, and considered a close confidant and friend, thought her a monster. There was no greater betrayal.

Margaret didn't feel she had anything to prove, but she laid off the girl's punishments for a while. She allowed her up during the day to play with the other children. The girls would make pillow forts in the parlor. She abhorred the mess, but Lucy's happiness was crucial. Plus, there was one other reason she chose to give the girl some leeway. She wanted to be back in Josie's good graces, and for whatever reason, Josie loved the girl.

The next great change occurred when Josie told her something incredibly troubling.

"Miss Margaret, I'm worried about Miss Lucy."

"Why? Is she sick?"

"No, ma'am," Josie hesitated before continuing. "Lucy told me this morning that the little girl is appearing to her again."

Margaret sighed. Lucy had a troubling imaginary playmate a couple of years before. She'd blamed this girl anytime she did anything naughty. The stage was not a pleasant one, but they'd heard nothing of this girl for quite a while. "What's brought this on?"

"I don't know, ma'am. But she told me this girl is instructing her to do bad things."

"Well, that's not new," Margaret laughed. "She used to take things all the time."

"I'm afraid this is worse than stealing sweets from the kitchens."

"Well, out with it. What is it, then?"

"She said this girl told her that the kitten doesn't have insides. She told her if she cut it open, she could see."

Margaret's blood ran cold. There was no way Lucy, her Lucy, could say such a horrific thing. "No. No, you're wrong. You misunderstood what she said."

"Miss Margaret, she asked me what the best thing would be to cut it open."

No. Margaret knew this was not Lucy. Lucy was sweet. Lucy loved animals. Her mind flashed back to the day of her youngest daughter's birth when she'd peered into the bassinet and seen how black her eyes were. She'd known then there was a demon inside her, and as soon as it got its opportunity, it would come for their family. She hadn't thought it would be so soon. Suddenly, she realized that Lucy first started seeing her imaginary friend right before the girl's birth. She couldn't believe she'd never connected the two events before. It now seemed painfully obvious.

"Is the kitten alive?" It wasn't a question she believed she'd ever need to ask. That fact was horrific all on its own.

"Yes, ma'am. I hid it in the attic. But that won't last long. She needs to see a doctor. Something is wrong with her."

"You hush your mouth," Margaret snarled at her. "There is nothing wrong with my baby. It's that other one. She's a bad influence, trying to get in Lucy's head."

"Miss Margaret, she can barely talk."

"I'm telling you it's her. And I'm afraid I can't allow her to

CHAPTER SIX

threaten my children. She'll have to stay in the cellar until she can learn to behave."

"Ma'am, it's bad enough she sleeps there unsupervised. For her to stay there constantly—"

"You do as you're told!" Margaret snapped again.

Josie admitted defeat and went off to find the girl and take her to the cellar.

As much as she wanted to get back into Josie's good graces, all their safety had to take top priority. The demon in this child was trying to make Lucy murder that innocent kitten. She knew the demon would not be satisfied with the kitten. It would then move to the family. She couldn't allow that.

Over the course of the next several months, Margaret felt her spirits lift more and more. With the girl in the cellar twenty-four/seven, it was often easy to forget she existed. Oh, she'd still cry and wail, particularly at night, but at least the sounds were muffled.

She started allowing Josie to take the girl food only once a day, then every other day. Food was scarce, and it needed to be saved for the family members. Not demons.

Margaret felt a great epiphany the day that she realized this was her test all along. She'd committed a horrible betrayal of John, and she needed to atone for it. She'd thought the soldiers that invaded the home had been her punishment. Then she'd thought it was the girl.

Now, she realized, he'd sent her a demon to banish. It was a personification of the sin she'd committed, and she needed to destroy it herself to make what she'd done right.

Starve the demon. Feed the girl. That was the only way. And the girl was buried deep within. She'd been too small to fight it out, considering it was there when she was born. Therefore, the body only needed the most basic of nourishment.

"Mama?" Lucy asked her one day while they were all around the dinner table.

"Yes, Lucy?"

"Where is my sister? She's hungry too."

Margaret set down her knife and fork and reached out her hand to take Lucy's. "Lucy, my dear, I know you care about her, but she's dangerous. You are not to play with her anymore. Do you hear me? You have no sister."

"But—"

"No! No sister. You must not mention her again. If you do, she'll kill you."

Percy set down his knife and studied his plate closely.

"Am I wrong?" she snapped at him.

His eyes flicked up to hers and then back to his plate. "No, ma'am. I don't want to play with stinky girls anyway."

"Good." Margaret smirked and glanced back at Lucy. "Remember. You must not speak of her again. You must not acknowledge her if you do see her, which you shouldn't. If you do, she'll kill you."

Then she picked her knife and fork back up and returned to eating.

CHAPTER SEVEN

Remi

"Remi. Remi, wake up." Richard's voice roused her from the dream, and she rolled over to return his stare.

"What time is it?"

"It's after seven," he answered. His voice was more clipped than normal. Great. He was still mad at her. "Everyone's in the kitchen for the meeting."

His eyes softened a bit as he studied her face. "Why are you crying, babe?"

She hadn't noticed the wetness on her cheeks until he'd mentioned it, but they chilled her skin almost instantly. She reached her hand up and wiped a tear away. "I don't know."

Richard wasn't convinced. He narrowed his eyes at her, but he didn't confront her. "Alright. Well come on down when you're ready. Natalie said we have something important to discuss."

He didn't wait for her response before leaving the room. Remi sat up in bed and wiped the rest of the tears away from her cheeks and stared into the mirror across from the bed.

Her hair was a tangled rat's nest that sat at a crooked angle on top of her head and her eyes were completely bloodshot.

Remi shot out of the bed and approached the mirror, as if pressing right up against the glass would change the reflection. Her eyes were beyond bloodshot. There was no white visible anymore. Had she really been crying that hard in her sleep? Why was she crying in the first place?

She squeezed her eyes shut and tried to remember. She knew she'd had another dream, but she couldn't remember any of the details. Like all the times before, except for that morning. Her heart wasn't pumping the way it normally did following those dreams, so she doubted it was a nightmare. It still had to be something significant though. She'd been bawling her eyes out. Why couldn't she remember?

Remi pressed her knuckles into her temples and rubbed them hard, trying to will the memory to the surface of her mind.

Oh well. Remi grabbed her hairbrush and pulled it violently through the knots in her hair. She didn't even wince when she pulled strands out by the roots. All she could think about was the dream and the way it evaded her. It was such an unsettling feeling. Hopefully, Natalie would be able to tell her what it was.

Remi poked her head in the nursery on the way downstairs and found the crib empty. The kids must be down there too. When she got to the kitchen, she was surprised. There was a full spread on the table, Emily was perched in her highchair, and Jessie cradled Kylie in her arms. Jessie hardly ever sat in on the meetings. They didn't have a problem with her. Quite the opposite. They were proud of her for turning her life around and doing so well. But when her shift was over, she preferred to leave, and they all respected that.

"You look lousy, doll," Natalie said when she saw her.

"Thanks." Remi took a seat next to Richard, who pointedly didn't look directly at her.

"So, what's going on?" he asked Natalie.

"I think we should wait for Gus. He's finishing up with a guest."

"Does it concern him?"

"It could potentially concern all of us."

As if on cue, Gus entered from the dining room carrying a frame in his arms.

"Sorry I'm late," he told them. "I was dealing with a very upset guest. Please tell me this was a joke."

He turned the frame around so they could see what it was. It was the infamous oil painting of Lucy Blackwood. Back in the day, this painting had a habit of moving around on its own, and when it wasn't moving around, Lucy's bright blue eyes followed you from the canvas.

The painting hadn't moved from its designated spot since the battle three years ago. They'd hung all the portraits of the Blackwood family in the parlor after that day.

"What are you doing with that?" Richard asked.

"Guest brought it down. She said it was on her bed when she got back from the bathroom. She was very upset and wanted to know why we let ourselves into her room. Are you telling me none of you know about this?"

"Ooohh!" Emily exclaimed and pointed her tiny finger at the portrait. "Lucy! Lucy!"

Remi's heart dropped. It felt like the room was spinning around her. She put a hand on Emily's arm. "Emily, do you know her, baby?"

"Lucy friend!" she exclaimed again and jabbed her finger in that direction. "Told you real!"

Remi and Natalie exchanged a glance before turning their attention to Emily.

"Emily," Remi said slowly, "you told Mommy the girl was mean. Was Lucy mean to you?"

"Lucy has owie," Emily grabbed a fistful of pasta. "Her mommy hurt her."

There was a sharp intake of breath next to her and Richard rose to his feet.

Remi's heart was dangerously close to bursting out of her chest, but she needed to push forward.

"Emily. How is Lucy mean to you?"

"She says Mommy hurt me."

Remi felt a sting as if she'd been slapped. Emily didn't act scared. She said it in a matter-of-fact tone before stuffing her fistful of pasta in her mouth.

"Oh, my God," Richard exclaimed. He rushed around the side of the table and snatched Emily out of the highchair so quickly she let out a wail of protest.

Richard hugged her tight to his body and gave Remi a death glare over her shoulder.

"Richard?" Remi spoke in a small, even breath. "You can't be serious."

"Give me time to talk to her," he said and walked to the staircase.

"Daddy!" Emily exclaimed, reaching over his shoulder. "I's hungwy!"

But Richard didn't turn around. He rushed up the stairs like there was a fire under his butt.

Remi swung her head back to face the others. "Is he serious

CHAPTER SEVEN

right now? She didn't even say I hurt her. Lucy did. Kids say crazy shit. We all know that. Right?"

Gus and Jessie exchanged a glance and shifted uncomfortably in their seats.

"It was a shock," Natalie told her soothingly. "Give him a little bit to calm down. It'll be alright."

Remi nodded, but she wasn't so sure what her friend said was true. Her husband acted as if she hurt their daughter. Honestly, if the shoe were on the other foot, she'd probably think the same thing and react. Why would Emily say that? Nothing about this made any sense.

Remi sighed and sat back in her chair.

"What does this mean?" Jessie asked quietly. One of her fingers was being tightly squeezed in Kylie's grip.

Natalie gestured for Gus to set the portrait against the wall and join them at the table, which he did.

Natalie blew out her breath before continuing. "I'll be honest here. The situation took a change from what I called you all about before. I asked everyone here because Remi's been having dreams about Margaret Blackwood and Emily was talking about a mean girl. Of course, now we know the mean girl is apparently Lucy. I was wondering if anyone else was experiencing anything else, *off*."

Gus shook his head. "Not until this." He gestured toward the portrait.

"Sometimes, I'll see shadows out of the corner of my eye," Jessie added. "When I look, nothing's there."

"You never said anything." Natalie told her.

Jessie shook her head. "I never had anything concrete."

Remi understood what she meant. When she'd spouted off about Blackwood Manor in the past, she'd found herself drugged to her eyeballs and locked in an institution. It made perfect sense she wouldn't want to say anything.

"Remi," Natalie said with a voice that was softer than normal for her and turned in her seat slightly, "when did Emily start talking about the mean girl?"

Remi leaned back and thought back. "Well, she started talking about a girl in her closet when I was in my first trimester with Kylie. But it was friendly. She seemed happy like she found a friend. We thought it was an imaginary playmate and didn't think anything of it. All kids have them. She started protesting going to bed a couple of weeks before Kylie was born, and she's been getting worse about it the longer it goes on. Last night was the first time she said anything about someone being mean to her. And now—-she's never said anything like that before."

Natalie nodded. "You said your dreams started when you were pregnant too?"

"Yeah. But I can never remember them when I wake up. Usually, I'm in a cold sweat and my heart's racing. This morning was the only time I could remember everything. I don't know why, but my gut feeling is the only reason I remembered that one was because Richard interrupted it."

Natalie nodded in agreement. "When I touched her this morning, I could see it too. There was only a black film when I tried to see the other dreams."

"What does that mean?" Remi asked.

"I don't know." Natalie bit her lip and studied a spot on the back wall. "That's unusual for me. It's like a mental block, but I don't have any clue what to make of that. I'm wondering if it's something to do with the dream realm."

Jessie scrunched up her eyebrows. "You can step beyond the

veil to the other side, but you can't enter the dream world?"

She was referring to the time Bailey possessed her while she was in the psychiatric hospital. Natalie posed as a maid to gain entry and come to see her. Upon meeting Jessie, she'd been able to go beyond the veil and have a conversation with Bailey.

Natalie shook her head. "That was different. Bailey pulled me in. She invited me. I've never done it on my own. If these dreams are being purposefully blocked, there's a reason."

"So, there's nothing we can do?" Remi sobbed.

"I didn't say that. I have to investigate things. It'll take a little time, but I'll figure it out. I promise."

"There's something I don't understand," Gus interrupted. "We used the haven stone to combat the evil. We broke the spell that Kate Wilkes put on the property, and all the spirits passed over. How can things be starting again now? It doesn't make sense."

"We'll figure it out," Natalie said again firmly. "I'll give Mel a call and see if she'll be willing to do a little research."

"How is she?" Remi asked, eager to change the subject.

"She's good. She got called back to that hotel she grew up in. I talked to her last year, and she said it was surreal being back there after so much time. I'll call her and see if she has any ideas of where to go from here. I'm also going to reach out to a few of my contacts who might know more about this dream thing. I really wish my grandma were still here."

Well, that answered that question. Remi had been about to ask if there was any way Natalie could contact her Grandma Sadie on the other side. The woman was a Seer when she was alive, and she'd once worked at Blackwood Manor. She would have been the perfect person to ask.

There was a ding from the front and Gus grinned in the

direction of the door. "I guess that's my cue," he said. "I'll talk to you guys later."

Remi turned to Jessie and stuck out her arms for the baby. "You go ahead and go on home, Jessie."

Jessie's jaw dropped. "Are you sure? I haven't done the laundry yet."

"It'll keep."

She meant it. Jessie had dark circles under her eyes, and she'd started shaking slightly throughout the meeting. Remi firmly believed that the girl needed a break from the house. The last thing she needed was another nervous breakdown.

Jessie said goodbye to Remi and Natalie before leaving for the day.

"Now, you," Natalie said, turning toward her. "You had another dream while you were upstairs, didn't you?"

Remi nodded.

"Do you know what it was about?"

"No, but I was crying when I woke up."

Natalie cupped Remi's face in her hands and closed her eyes. Remi stayed as still and silent as she could to give her friend the optimal chance to discover something.

Natalie shook her head and stepped away. "Nope. That one's blocked too."

"I'm scared, Nat."

"I know you are. But I don't want you to worry. I got you. We all do."

Remi accepted the hug before making her way up the servant's staircase. She peeked into Emily's bedroom on the way to the nursery and found Richard sitting on the edge of her bed, with their little girl tucked contentedly into his side. He grasped a story book in the other hand and looked up when

CHAPTER SEVEN

he heard the door open.

"Can I come in?" she asked quietly.

He nodded and she entered, gently rocking Kylie as she went.

"Look. I don't know what's going on, but I swear to God, I've never hurt either one of our girls. I could never."

"I know. She told me."

"She needed to tell you?"

There was an awkward silence before Richard spoke again. "It's just—you have been keeping things from me, Remi. Don't say you haven't. You don't look present half the time, you're not sleeping. You'll say you're going to class when I know you're not."

She hung her head with a pang of guilt as she remembered that morning.

"Dad! Read!" Emily punctuated each word with a hard stab of her finger to the book.

"Let's talk about this later, okay?"

"Sure." Remi didn't want to talk about it later, but the kids would always be top priority. That's something they'd always agreed on. No matter what, they would put a hold on their own issues and make sure the kids were taken care of. And Emily wanted a bedtime story.

"I'll be there in twenty," he told her.

"Read!" Emily hit the book again.

"Yeah." Remi turned and left the room with them both knowing he would not be in anytime soon.

CHAPTER EIGHT

Remi
2009

"It's not so bad," Remi's friend Delilah told her as they walked home from school. The two girls went to an elite private school together and lived on the same block. It was only natural that they'd become fast friends.

Remi hugged her books to her chest and bit her lip.

"Don't do that. You'll bruise." Delilah playfully nudged her shoulder as they walked.

Remi sighed. Of course it wasn't a big deal to Delilah. Delilah lived in a normal house with a normal family where she was allowed to be a kid. A ninety-five on a math test would be displayed on the refrigerator and she'd be taken out for ice cream later. A ninety-five looked very different for Remi.

"You missed one question," her friend said quietly.

One question. It might as well be one million.

They came to a stop on the sidewalk outside her house and dread bubbled up inside Remi's chest like red hot lava. She didn't want to go inside.

"He's gonna be mad," she mumbled under her breath.

CHAPTER EIGHT

"I don't know why," Delilah shrugged. "Everyone misses a question sometimes. It's not a big deal."

"Remi!"

She looked toward the house. Her father stood on the front porch dressed in an impeccably neat suit. "Did you get your math test back today?"

"Yes, Papa," she said in a squeaky voice.

"Come in the house. Let me see it."

"Yes, Papa."

"I need to get home anyway. See ya, sir!" Delilah waved before continuing down the sidewalk.

He nodded at her and waited for Remi to make her way up the steps and into the house.

She made for the stairs to take her belongings into her room.

"No," her father said simply. "No stalling. Come in here."

He took a seat in his favorite chair and gestured for Remi to sit on the sofa across from him.

"Let's have it." He stuck his hand out.

Remi set her schoolbooks on the coffee table and pulled her math folder out of her backpack. She handed her test to her father.

She held her breath as he looked down at the big, red "95" on the top.

He looked at her over the top of the page and grunted in frustration. "This is unacceptable, Remi. What did I tell you would happen if your grades didn't improve?"

"It did improve, Papa."

She wasn't lying. Her last test was a ninety-two. Math was her worst subject, and it drove her father insane.

"Don't you sass me," he hissed at her.

Remi averted her gaze to the ground and waited for him to mentally tear into her again.

"How do you expect to get into medical school with grades like that?"

Remi seriously doubted a ninety-five in third grade math would affect her chances, but she didn't say that. What she did say may have been an even bigger mistake. "I don't want to be a doctor."

"What did you say? And look at me when I'm talking to you."

Remi looked him straight in the eye. "I don't want to be a doctor," she repeated.

He glared at her without speaking. It was as if he were daring her to say more. She rose to the challenge. "I don't like blood. It makes me queasy."

"So, you'd rather sleep on the sidewalk somewhere? Because you don't like blood? Is that what you're telling me? I have news for you, young lady. Everyone has to do things they don't want to do. I don't want to hear another word about you not being a doctor. You know what this means, don't you? No music camp this summer."

Tears welled in her eyes. She'd worked hard to get into music camp. She played violin well and was able to express herself through her music. It was her only joy. "But Papa!" she exclaimed, "I worked so hard!"

He sneered at her. "Well, if you put as much effort into your math, you'd still be able to go."

"What if I get a perfect score on my next test?"

He shook his head. "Absolutely not. I gave you an opportunity to improve your grade and you didn't. I won't keep renegotiating. You'll never learn that way. No music camp this summer. Maybe this will motivate you to stay on top of your work. Maybe next year."

Remi hated the tears that streamed down her face, but she couldn't help it. She didn't know why her father hated her so much, but she was convinced he did. Nothing she did was right. She'd be criticized

CHAPTER EIGHT

for things her friend's families praised. It didn't make any sense to her.

* * *

Remi looked down at Kylie, who was cradled in her arms. The baby fell asleep while nursing, and now there was the tiniest line of milk dribbling out of her mouth.

Remi readjusted her shirt to cover her breast and carried Kylie to the crib before carefully lowering her inside. Her mind thought back to that horrible memory of the day she realized she'd never be good enough. One third grade math test did so much to break her spirit. She'd struggled for years with low self-esteem and self-worth because she knew, no matter how well she did, she'd always be expected to do better.

There was a knock on the door and Gus stuck his head in. "Excuse me, Remi. There are people here asking for you by name."

"Who are they?"

"They wouldn't say."

Remi rolled her eyes but proceeded to follow Gus down to the first floor. She hated unexpected visitors. It was incredibly rude to show up unannounced in her opinion, and she really wasn't up for visitors. She nearly fell down the last three steps when she saw who was standing in the foyer.

Her mother awkwardly stood in the doorway to the parlor with a suitcase clasped in both hands in front of her. Her father was clearly surveying the surrounding area.

"What are you doing here?" Remi asked them, shocked.

Her father put his hands on his hips and glared at her. "So, this is what you threw away your life for?"

Here we go, Remi thought to herself. He's graduated to flying across the country to insult me. But what is he doing here? She hadn't spoken to them in years, and when she'd moved to Georgia, she hadn't told them.

Remi couldn't help but be annoyed that he was turning his nose up at the place already. Their bed & breakfast was very profitable. She could have understood this reaction a few years ago, but now the place was bright, homey, and impeccably decorated.

"I'm hardly throwing my life away," she said coldly. "We do quite well for ourselves, and I'm top of my class in medical school."

Her father looked at her up and down and sneered. "Might have known you'd let yourself go."

Heat warmed her cheeks. "I had a baby five weeks ago."

Her father chuckled. "That figures."

Her mother, however, broke into a wide smile. "A baby!" she exclaimed. "I have a grandchild?"

Remi nodded. "Two, actually."

Her mother beamed, but Remi felt no affection. Her mother was always good with children, but she'd never done much to stick up for Remi when she was being insulted, and that was something that couldn't be forgiven.

"Why are you here?" Remi repeated.

"I have a work conference in Savannah for the next six weeks," he told her. "Since that would be quite an expensive stay, and we have a daughter so close, it made more sense to come here."

CHAPTER EIGHT

Remi's heart was in her stomach. She didn't want them here, but their business was about giving people a place to stay. She couldn't very well turn them away without just cause. "Well, we stay pretty busy." She turned to Gus. "Do we have anything available?"

He checked the spreadsheet before answering. "We're booked in full for the next three weeks. We'll have an opening after that for about four days. There was a cancellation."

Thank God. Remi shrugged and turned back to her father. "I'm afraid we're full. You're free to book the empty slot if you want, but it may not be worth it, being it's only for four days."

Her father turned his lips up in a sneer she wanted to slap off his face. "You're telling me in a house this big, there's nowhere to put us?"

"The rooms are all full," she repeated slowly. She thought of the irony. He spent her entire childhood making her feel as if she were stupid, but he couldn't seem to understand such a simple concept.

"You don't have family quarters?"

"We do, but there are only three rooms."

"Then what's the problem? You said you have two children, correct? Simply put the children together and there is room right there. I swear, Remi, you never did see what was right in front of your face."

"I am not putting a newborn baby in with a toddler," she said through clenched teeth. "Besides, I hardly think the two of you will be comfortable in a toddler bed."

"Don't be ridiculous. We'll be in your room, of course. We are the guests."

"Now, wait one minute," Remi snapped.

"Remi?" Richard called her name as he came down the stairs.

Her father looked him up and down in his jeans and oversized work shirt. "What's going on?"

"We're Remi's parents," her father interjected before she could speak.

"Oh, it's so nice to meet you finally!" Richard broke out into a big grin and reached for his father-in-law's hand, seemingly unaware of the sour look on the man's face. "I'm Richard, Remi's husband."

Her father turned his gaze back to Remi and glared hard. "Husband, is he?"

"You didn't tell me they were coming, babe," Richard smiled at her.

"I didn't know," she told him with a clipped voice.

"No, no. We surprised her, I'm afraid." Her father laughed. "See, I have a work event in Savannah and will be here for a few weeks. When her cousin, Naomi, found out, she suggested we stay here. She told us all about the bed & breakfast."

"And as I was telling him," Remi hissed, never taking her eyes off her father, "we're booked solid for the next three weeks."

"We can move Emily into the nursery," Richard shrugged.

"That's a horrible idea, Richard," she snapped at him. "Emily's having issues sleeping and it will disturb the baby. Neither of them will get any sleep."

"It's only for a little bit. They're family."

"He's right, Remi," her father said. "We're family."

"It'll take us a little bit to get everything moved around," Richard smiled. "If you're not in too big of a hurry, you can go into the dining room and order something for lunch, on the house. Tell Jessie I approved it. Hopefully by the time you've finished, we'll have worked something out."

Her father nodded his agreement. "That'll be fine. At least

one of you is hospitable." He shot his daughter another glare before walking into the dining room.

Richard took the suitcase from his mother-in-law, and she followed her husband.

Remi grabbed his arm and dragged him into the parlor.

"Why did you do that? I was trying to get them to leave."

He scrunched up his eyebrows. "Why would you want your parents to leave?"

"Has it escaped your attention that they weren't at our wedding? Or that you've never even met them in all the time we've known each other?"

"I thought they couldn't make it."

"We're not on speaking terms. I don't want them here!"

"Why?"

"It doesn't matter. It's too late now!" she threw her hands up in the air. "You overrode my no, so you can rearrange everything. They expect our bed."

She shoved past him and ran up the stairs.

CHAPTER NINE

Remi

When Remi came downstairs that evening, she felt like she was headed to her own funeral. The others thought she was being crazy, another thing to add to the ever-growing resume. Apparently, her parents were downright pleasant during lunch. So, no one understood her reaction to them being here.

She knew they were playing nice to worm their way in, and that it would be very short-lived. She'd called her lovely cousin Naomi to chew her out for telling them where to find her, but all she'd gotten was voicemail. That conversation would be coming very soon.

Thankfully, right after lunch her father went into Savannah for a meeting, and her mother went with him to explore the city. That was fine with Remi.

She'd taken off with the girls. She went to the park, then they'd gone to Sophia's house for hours. This wasn't something she'd be able to keep up for six weeks. She knew that.

When they'd returned to the house, her parents still hadn't

CHAPTER NINE

come back yet. Thank God for that. She still hadn't been ready to see them. Richard followed her up the stairs and explained the new arrangements. He'd moved Emily's bed into the nursery, as well as her toy box. He'd then gone into town to buy a queen-sized blow-up mattress for the two of them and put it in Emily's room. He'd put her parents' suitcase into their room.

"It's only temporary, of course," he told her. "I ordered a new mattress online. It'll be here in a couple of days." They'd recently put their last spare mattress into one of the rooms. The previous residents of that room had snuck a dog in that peed all over the mattress, and they didn't bother to report it before leaving. It had been beyond cleaning.

"Uh huh," Remi grunted noncommittally. She'd moved from room to room, putting Kylie in the crib for a nap, running a bath for Emily, and went into their room, it was still their room—she refused to refer to it as her parents', and removed anything of value that she didn't want them sneaking through.

"Don't you think that's a bit dramatic?" Richard asked.

"Nope," she answered before returning to the bathroom to assist Emily.

Now it was time for dinner. She had Emily perched on her hip as she entered the dining room. Normally, they ate in the kitchen to keep the dining room in tip-top shape for the guests, but two tables had been pushed together and set. The guests had already eaten, and now it was their turn.

"Oh!" her mother exclaimed and clapped her hands when she saw them. She rushed forward with her arms outstretched.

Emily squealed and buried her face in her mother's neck. Remi stuck out a palm to stop her mother. "She's scared of strangers. We'll need to ease her into this."

Her father snorted from his spot at the dining room window. "Yet you run a bed & breakfast."

God, this was going to be a rough six weeks. Remi bit the inside of her cheek until she tasted blood before responding, "Well, it's not as if the guests try to handle my children."

"Hey, babe," Richard and Jessie entered from the kitchen carrying plates that they placed on the tables. "Dinner is served."

Remi slipped Emily into her highchair and took the seat directly next to her so she could circumvent any unwanted attention.

Her father's eyebrows pinched together when he saw that Gus and Jessie were sitting down with them. "I assumed with it being our first night it would be family."

"They are family," Remi snapped before grabbing the dish of chicken that was closest to her on the table. She passed it to Richard. It was only a small slight toward her parents, but it still made her feel good for a few seconds. She'd take it.

"Who you?" Emily asked, crossing her tiny arms in front of her. She wasn't impressed. Remi couldn't help but be proud. Mama didn't raise an idiot.

"This is your grandma and grandpa, honey," Richard smiled looking at them.

Remi pitied her husband. She understood his excitement. He'd lost his family when he was eight years old, and all he'd ever wanted was family. Having a mother and father figure walk into his life probably was a dream come true to him. But he didn't know how it was going to end up. They would end up being suffocated, and she wouldn't be surprised if Richard was driven to start drinking again.

"Should we all call you grandma and grandpa?" Gus joked.

CHAPTER NINE

Remi knew where he was coming from. They'd never properly introduced themselves. They'd only said they were her parents.

Her father glared at him. "No. You may call us Mr. and Mrs. Huang. Because Richard is now our son, he may either call us Mama and Papa or Malaki and Mira."

There was a moment of silence before a yell of "yoo-hoo!" rang through the house. Natalie bounded into the room eliciting a haughty look from Malaki.

"Oh, what's the occasion?" Natalie plopped down in the seat next to Remi.

"Do you not knock, young lady?" Malaki asked.

Natalie gave him a long look before sarcastically smiling. "I'm sorry. Who are you?"

"Natalie, these are Remi's parents Malaki and Mira Huang." Richard introduced them.

"Natalie is a very close friend," Remi cut in. "She also works here part time."

"I repeat, do you not knock?"

Natalie smiled wider. "It's a bed & breakfast, dear. No one knocks. If that bothers you, you may want to find other accommodations."

"Excuse me?"

"Well, it seems to me you are extremely uncomfortable with the arrangements here. That's okay. The set up is not for everyone."

"So," Richard interjected before Malaki could pop back off, "you're not on shift. What brings you by?"

"I came to report on what we talked about earlier."

Remi caught her eye and shook her head ever so slightly. Thankfully, her friend seemed to catch her meaning because she didn't elaborate.

There was a ding from the front, and Natalie looked in that direction. "I got it. You all enjoy your meal."

"What was she talking about, Remi?" Malaki asked when Natalie left the room.

"Some history on the house," Remi lied and dug into her plate.

* * *

After dinner, when Remi led her parents into their new room, she bit her cheek to keep control over herself.

Mira immediately went to the dresser and began transferring items from their suitcase. Malaki walked the room, examining every surface.

"Your husband is not the type one would expect for a girl of your upbringing," he said to her as he wiped his fingers across the windowsill, "but he at least has a better sense of family values than you do. Your friends, however, are vulgar."

"Well, they're not going anywhere," she said through clenched teeth.

He sneered. "We'll see."

They leveled their eyes on each other in an awkward stare down. "Richard does have potential. We'll have to see to getting him some training."

"You leave my husband alone," she growled through gritted teeth.

He sneered before continuing. "I require my breakfast at

CHAPTER NINE

five in the morning. I trust you remember what I take?"

"Breakfast is served at seven. You may eat in the dining room with everyone else. You'll eat what we serve."

"That's not acceptable. I have to be in Savannah by seven."

"Well, that's too bad," she hissed. "I have a class in the morning, I don't have time to make you a special breakfast, and it's not the staff's responsibility, either. I won't push it off on them. If our breakfast accommodations are not acceptable for you, you'll need to get your breakfast on your way to work."

Remi turned on her heel and was about to walk out the door when her mother called out to her.

"Remi?"

"Yes, Mama?" Remi answered without turning around.

"Where is the bathroom?"

"Down the hall on the right. Towels are in the closet."

Without waiting for a reply, Remi left the room and rushed to Emily's room, closing the door behind her.

Richard was rearranging some of Emily's small furniture to make it easier for them to maneuver. He looked up when she entered. He flicked his eyes down to Emily, who sat on the mattress playing with a doll, and back up to rest on Remi.

"Are you okay?"

"No," she sighed. "He's already trying to take over."

"Well, he's got a strong personality," Richard shrugged. "I wouldn't say he's trying to take over."

"Richard, stop it." Remi put a hand up to stop him. "I'm the one that grew up with him. I know his idiosyncrasies and the way his mind works. He came in here being insulting, demanding our bedroom, and trying to lecture our friends. I don't like it. This is the beginning."

"Mean man," Emily chimed in.

They both looked at her.

"What do you mean, sweetheart?" Remi asked.

"Lucy says mean man make Mommy mean."

Remi and Richard exchanged a look but didn't verbally comment on it. Remi sat on the edge of the bed before speaking once more. "I really wish you hadn't invited them here."

"I didn't invite them," he sat on the floor and took her hand. "They were already here. I didn't turn them away. You can't do that to family."

"Richard, you know how you feel about your uncle?"

He flinched, and Remi felt a flicker of guilt for hitting that sore spot. She didn't know how else she could get her point across. Richard was sent to live with an abusive uncle after his parents died.

"Well, that's how I feel about my father. Mom too, to a lesser degree."

He scrunched up his eyebrows in confusion. "I don't understand. You had everything growing up."

"Everything but a loving family."

Richard cocked his head to the side.

"Shit, I'm not explaining this well," she ran her hands through her hair.

"Mommy! Bad word!" Emily scolded.

"I'm sorry, baby," Remi patted Emily's head before turning back to Richard. "Yeah, I grew up in a nice house, went to a fancy private school, and didn't have to worry about basic necessities. I understand how that's bliss compared to the way you grew up, but all those material things don't equate happiness."

"So, what happened?"

CHAPTER NINE

"The pressure was unreal. I had to be perfect, and it was unacceptable to be a child. I would be punished for the smallest infractions."

"Did he—"

"No, he never hit me." She shook her head. "But sometimes I wish he had. I think it would have been easier. A wrinkle in my clothes? Give away my cat. Don't get a perfect score on a math test? No music camp that I worked months to be ready for. It was decided I would be a doctor before I was six years old. Anytime I voiced any other ambition, I was told I'd end up on the street. My clothes were chosen for me. The boys I dated were chosen for me. My friends were chosen for me.

"I wasn't even allowed to have my own hobby. Everything was predetermined. At one point, I literally had nothing in my bedroom except for my bed. I purposefully moved away and cut contact. Cousins told me they asked questions for a while, but eventually it died away. I thought I'd never have to deal with them again."

There was a knock on the door, and Natalie stuck her head in. "Can I come in?"

Remi nodded. Natalie entered the room and sat cross-legged on the floor. Emily shot to her feet and raced to plop herself in Natalie's lap.

"So, I didn't say much downstairs. I kind of got the vibe this wasn't something we should talk about in front of your parents."

"Oh, no," Remi agreed, and sighed. "What did you find?"

"I called Mel. She'll come as soon as she can. She did tell me there have been documented cases of curses similar to Rebecca's being dormant, but not actually broken. We think that's what's happening with the sudden weird stuff starting to happen."

"So, what makes it not dormant anymore?" Richard asked.

"Residual energy, probably," Natalie said as she ran a hand through Emily's hair. "Normally an event that mirrors something that happened in the past."

"But what—" Remi broke off and raised a trembling hand to her mouth. The light bulb went off in her head. She looked at Emily, and her mind raced with the things she'd been saying recently about Lucy, and their mommies. "Kylie's birth?" she squeaked.

Richard grabbed her hand and squeezed it tight. "How do we get ahead of this?"

"Don't you two go jumping to any conclusions," Natalie wagged a finger at them. "We don't know anything for sure. But the timing did make Mel voice the theory. She's going to do more research and come back when she's done with her current project."

"Where is she?" Richard thundered. "We need her now."

"She went back to Hotel Dahlia. Something happened. She didn't give me any details."

Hotel Dahlia was the hotel Mel grew up in. It was haunted and fueled her interest in history and research. They had her past there to thank for much of the investigation going the way it did three years ago. As far as Remi knew, she hadn't been back there in years.

"In the meantime," Natalie continued, "I sent an email to Nadine Lewis."

Richard sighed. "Nadine Lewis?"

Nadine Lewis was a medium that Richard's aunt Claire hired back in 2009. She'd only done a single walkthrough, and Claire didn't invite her back. The woman was commercial and even had one of those call-in psychic hotlines. Not wanting a media circus, his family decided not to use her services. If they didn't want her, Richard didn't want her.

Natalie put her hands up. "Before you get loopy, hear my reason. Nadine has been in the house; she told your aunt something. She may know something that could be beneficial. Her hotline has been out of service for years, and she's mainly out of the public eye now. It wouldn't be the media travesty it would have been back then."

"Okay," Richard sighed. "But I reserve the right to ask her to leave."

"Of course. If she gets too gimmicky, she's out of here. Well, I better get back home to Dani." Natalie turned her gaze to Remi. "How long are your parents going to be here?"

Remi hung her head. "They say six weeks."

"Do you want them to know about everything that's going on?"

"I would prefer not to, but I don't know how long we can keep it a secret. I mean, if the house is waking up…"

"Well, we'll try to keep it low key for now. I'll talk to you guys later." They told Natalie good night and began getting ready for bed.

CHAPTER TEN

Margaret

Margaret was astonished the day she looked out the kitchen window and saw Josie digging a hole on the grounds. She gathered her skirts in her hands to avoid tripping on them and rushed out the door toward her.

Josie sobbed hysterically as she hit the ground repeatedly with her shovel. A small, burlap sack sat at her feet.

"Josie! What the devil are you doing?"

Josie dropped to her knees and dragged a quivering hand across her cheek. "I have to bury it."

"You have to bury what?"

Josie didn't answer, but her eyes flickered to the sack.

Margaret snatched it, reached her hand inside, and pulled out the contents.

She held Lucy's kitten. It was dead. She carefully examined it but found no cuts or slices. She saw no apparent cause of death. "What happened to it?"

Josie's fists dug into the earth, her fingers holding tight to the grass.

CHAPTER TEN

"Answer me!" Margaret demanded, grasping Josie by the shoulders and shaking her.

"I found Miss Lucy with it this morning. In the washing basin."

Margaret's heart thundered dangerously. She was getting tired of these heartless accusations of her baby. She nearly snapped at Josie, but she couldn't ignore the distress in the other woman's body. She shook and cried harder than Margaret ever saw. Even worse than when the soldiers came. No, she wasn't lying. She'd witnessed this kitten murdered.

"Maybe she found it," Margaret didn't recognize her own voice as she spoke. She didn't want to believe this of her precious daughter. Lucy couldn't have done this. She was the sweet one. It wasn't possible! She tenderly ran her hands over the kitten once again and couldn't deny that her chest and abdominal cavity were already swollen and bloated.

Josie shook her head. "She was holding it under. When I asked her why, she said—she said she wanted to see how long it could breathe."

Margaret's head spun and her knees shook. What? No. This wasn't happening.

"She said the girl told her it would stop and then come back as a lion."

The girl again! The demon! Of course, that was what happened. Margaret moved to go back to the house and confront the girl. Then everything went dark, and she crumpled to the ground.

"Miss Margaret! Miss Margaret!" Josie's fingers tapped lightly on her cheeks, bringing her around.

Margaret opened her eyes and squinted against the sun above her. She was lying flat on her back outside. Why was she out here?

She took Josie's offered hand and sat up slowly as her back ached in protest. "What happened?"

"You fainted."

Margaret surveyed her surroundings and noticed the burlap sack laying a few feet away. It all came back to her. "The girl," she growled.

"Miss Lucy is the one who drowned the kitten," Josie said firmly.

"Because the girl told her to," Margaret insisted.

Josie stared at her and shook her head in disbelief.

Margaret's cheeks reddened in embarrassment. The nerve of Josie to doubt what she said! "Fine," she said simply. "Let's ask her, shall we?"

Margaret got to her feet and moved toward the house. "Josie!" she called when she noticed the other woman was not behind her.

There was a rustling of skirts and Josie followed her inside.

When they entered through the kitchen door, Margaret was immediately met with the sound of the children playing in the parlor. She made her way toward their voices, making sure that Josie was close behind. She wanted the woman to hear what she knew was the truth.

"Percy! Play with me!" Lucy begged.

"No. You're a freak," her brother hissed.

When Margaret reached the parlor door she was met with another one of Lucy's pillow and blanket forts. "Lucy, sit down," she ordered.

Her daughter turned toward her, and the smile fell from her beautiful face. She hated that she elicited such a response from her baby, but she needed to get to the bottom of what was going on.

"Josie showed me the kitten," Margaret said once Lucy took her place on the loveseat.

Her daughter looked at the floor. That was a pet peeve for Margaret. She snapped her fingers in front of Lucy's face and made her jump. "Look at me when I'm talking to you."

Lucy looked at her with tear-filled eyes.

"Josie said she saw you holding the kitten under at the water basin. Is that the truth?"

Lucy's lip quivered and a sob escaped her.

"Answer me. Is that the truth?"

"Yes, ma'am," Lucy said quietly.

"Why would you do something like that?"

"The girl in my closet told me to."

"Do not lie to me."

"I'm not!" Lucy sighed and tears rolled freely down her face. "I know you say she isn't real, but she is. She has long, dark hair and blue eyes. She told me I had a special kitten. That it was magical and would come back to life as a lion who would protect us all against evil."

Margaret was growing increasingly annoyed. She'd expected Lucy to tell her that wretched little girl was behind this. But she was describing a dark-haired girl. "How old is this girl?"

"I don't know. Old. Thirteen, I guess."

"What is her name?"

"She never told me."

Margaret pinched the bridge of her nose and took a deep breath. It was taking everything she had to not lose her temper.

"Lucy, you are getting too old to blame imaginary friends when you do something wrong."

"She's not imaginary!" Lucy shouted indignantly. "She lives in my closet, and she tells me things. She tells me about how this land is cursed, and we have to help all the souls here. She tells me you're going mad!"

"Maybe she is real," Percy said under his breath.

Margaret's head swung toward her son and he quickly looked to the floor.

"You two go to your rooms. I'm tired of your lies."

"But Mama!"

"Now!"

Her two children stomped to the staircase grumbling at each other.

Margaret tore a blanket from the fort and tossed it across the room before collapsing into a chair. Josie tentatively stepped forward and sat opposite her.

"What are we going to do?"

Margaret thought hard. She'd heard of an orphanage outside of Atlanta, but getting the girl there would be problematic. She couldn't send Josie. She would inevitably be detained on the way, and if she went herself, she'd have to admit it was her child. That was the last thing she wanted.

"Do you know of anyone I can pay to discreetly take her to the orphanage?" Margaret quietly asked.

Josie cocked her head to the side. "Ma'am?"

"The girl!" Margaret threw up her hands in exasperation.

"I was talking about Miss Lucy."

"Excuse me?"

"You heard her. She needs help."

"That's what I'm doing," Margaret spoke slowly. Why was this so difficult to understand? "I want to send away the problem so nothing like this ever happens again. But we have to do it in a way that can't be tied back to me."

"She said it was a teenage girl with dark hair."

"She's clearly lying. She wants to protect the girl. For some reason, she likes her."

Josie shook her head. "She's not. She's been talking about this closet girl since before the child was born."

"Do not argue with me!" Margaret spat. "I'm her mother. I will say what's what! Now, do you know anyone who can take her or not?"

"I do not."

"Well, ask around the next time you go into town."

"And why should I say I'm asking these questions?"

Margaret jumped to her feet and stomped toward the doorway. "I don't know!" she screamed over her shoulder. "Figure it out! Do I have to do everything?"

CHAPTER ELEVEN

Remi

A scream cut through the night, causing Remi to shoot out of bed before she was fully awake.

"Remi?" Richard asked groggily next to her, but she didn't stop to talk. The terrified scream thundered in her head, and she raced down the hall to the nursery.

When she busted through the door, her mother stood next to the crib holding Kylie. "Shh. It's Grammy, angel," she whispered to Emily, who sat in the corner on her toddler mattress with tears streaming down her face.

Without thinking, Remi strode across the room and snatched Kylie out of her mother's arms. "What the fuck do you think you're doing in here?" she spat.

Mira took a step back as if Remi struck her. "I—the baby was crying. I came in to check on her."

"That's bullshit!" Remi screamed.

Richard and Malaki both ambled into the room, rubbing their tired eyes. "What's going on?" Richard asked.

Remi ignored him and continued to scream at her mother. "We have a baby monitor in our room. Plus, she sleeps through the night. If anyone was crying it would have been Emily!" Kylie was not sleeping through the night yet. But that wasn't the point. The rest was still valid.

"Lower your voice when you're talking to your mother," Malaki growled.

"Shut up! I'm not talking to you!" Remi shook with rage and returned her gaze to her mother. "Let me make one thing perfectly clear right now. This is our house and our children. You will not wander around as you please. You will stay away from our girls."

"They are our grandchildren. We have a right to see them," Malaki said simply. "We're under the same roof. It is inevitable."

"You can see them in the dining room with everyone else. Under no circumstances will you come into their bedroom. Especially not in the middle of the night."

"We will go where we please."

"GET OUT!" Remi screamed at the top of her lungs.

Emily squealed in the corner and put her hands over her ears. "Stop yelling! Stop yelling!"

Kylie was crying in her arms now, but Remi did not back down. She stomped her foot and stared down her parents. "Get out! Get out!"

"Remi, baby," Richard stepped forward and put a soothing hand on her shoulder. "Let's all calm down and go back to bed. It's been a busy day."

"I'm not leaving this room!" she hissed. "Don't you see? The first chance they got, they came in here and invaded our girl's space. I'm sleeping here tonight."

"Okay, okay." Richard tenderly pushed her hair out of her eyes and turned back to Malaki and Mira. "Guys, I think you better go on back to bed."

"She is acting like a lunatic," Malaki screamed. "A baby cries, you go to them. That's all Mira was doing."

"We didn't hear it," Richard said patiently, "even though we do have a baby monitor. It would scare any mother to find someone in her child's bedroom in the middle of the night. I think we all need some rest. We can talk about it tomorrow." He put a hand on his father-in-law's shoulder, much as he'd done to Remi moments before.

"I suppose you're right," Malaki stepped back but gave Remi a hard look. "But we will be talking about your disrespect tomorrow." He slipped an arm around Mira's shoulders, and they left the nursery. Richard closed the door behind them and turned back to Remi.

"Don't you think that was a bit of an overreaction?"

Remi shook her head. "Something was wrong about the whole thing." She sunk down onto the toddler mattress and pulled a sobbing Emily into her side with her free hand.

"Are you okay, baby? Did she hurt you?"

Emily shook her head. "Lucy say she take me away. She take baby Kywee away."

Remi shot concerned eyes to Richard.

He lowered himself to his knees and took Emily's hands in his. "Lucy said this? Tonight?"

Emily nodded. "Before mean lady came." She hiccupped.

"Where is Lucy now?"

Emily looked over his shoulder and they followed her gaze.

It was a good thing Remi was sitting down because her knees weakened, and her head spun. The bedroom door was now slightly ajar, and Lucy Blackwood stood in the doorway looking in at them.

CHAPTER ELEVEN

She'd seen Lucy before, of course. But that was three years ago. At the time, she'd been terrifying despite her small stature. Blue scaly skin and horns atop her head. She'd also been a vicious little thing. They thought she'd left with all the rest of the spirits when they'd battled Heaven's Estate.

Now, here she was standing merely a few feet away, but her presence was different somehow. She didn't have a lurking, menacing air about her now. She looked like a little girl. Yes, her skin still had a slightly blue tint to it, but the scales were gone. There were no horns on her head, but there were red marks where they'd once been. The dead giveaway that she was Lucy was the dark stain of blood on her nightgown.

Richard shot to his feet and used his body to block his wife and children. "What are you doing back here?"

Lucy didn't answer. A tear rolled down her cheek.

A tear? How could that be possible? Was it possible for a ghost to cry?

Remi was filled with sorrow at the sight of the crying child before her. Loneliness and pain coursed through her from the tips of her toes, all the way to her cheeks, and she began to cry herself. Something was different now. But Remi knew Lucy didn't want to hurt them.

Without saying a word, Lucy turned and disappeared down the dark hallway.

CHAPTER TWELVE

Remi

Remi didn't sleep at all that night. When she finally plodded down to the kitchen in the morning, she stopped short at the sight of her mother washing dishes.

Mira plopped the plate she was holding back into the water and blushed. "Is it alright that I'm in here? Your father wanted his breakfast before his meeting."

Remi nodded. "As long as you clean up after yourself. Has he already left?"

"Yes. He got a cab about five minutes ago."

Some of the tension left Remi's body and she made her way to the coffee pot.

"Remi," Mira carefully began, "I want to apologize for last night. While I do think your reaction was slightly overboard, I understand."

Remi brought her mug to her lips and blew on the liquid to cool it. She looked at her mother, waiting for her to go on.

"You were right. I shouldn't have been in your children's bedroom. I may be your mother, but we haven't seen each

CHAPTER TWELVE

other in years, and I'm a stranger to those girls. When the oldest woke up and saw me in her room, it scared her something awful. I feel so guilty about that."

"So, why did you go in there? Did you really hear the baby crying?"

"Yes, but—" Mira broke off and bit her lip.

"Go on."

Mira looked both ways as if checking to make sure no one else could hear her. "Remi, I don't want you to think I'm insulting you or your way of life, but I think something is very wrong about this place."

A chill ran down Remi's spine, but she would not show any sign of weakness around her mother. It would be a recipe for disaster.

"Why do you say that?" she asked.

"It was a strange feeling at first," Mira admitted. "A heaviness in the air, shadows moving in the corner of my eye. But then last night, I did hear the baby crying. I swear it. I didn't even think. I got up and went to her. But when I got there, the crying was coming from the baby, but her mouth wasn't open."

"What are you talking about?"

"Her mouth was closed like she was asleep, but the crying was coming from her body. And her eyes were black."

No weakness. Don't show weakness.

"This house can mess with your head when you're not used to it," she finally said. "I think it comes down to how old the place is. It does have odd creaks and strange shadows sometimes. I think you misinterpreted what you saw."

Mira nodded. "Of course. You're right. I don't know what I was thinking."

Remi set her coffee mug in the sink. "If you'll excuse me, I have to go get dressed for my class."

"Of course."

"One more thing. You said Emily was asleep when you went in the room?"

"I'm sorry, which one is Emily?"

"The oldest."

"Yes. She was asleep. When she woke up and saw me, she got scared and started crying."

"Thank you."

Remi went upstairs and began getting ready for school. She didn't know how she'd managed to keep her cool with her mother downstairs and stay so nonchalant, but the truth was she was terrified by her mom's story. She didn't have any reason to doubt what she said. No one mentioned the house's haunted history to her parents. But she was bothered by the discrepancy in her and Emily's stories. Had the child been asleep or not?

***

"*Remi*," Sophia hissed and pinched her arm.

Remi jolted awake. "What?" she halfway shouted.

Her vision cleared, and she saw that she was at her desk in class. Everyone in the room turned to look at her, a few of them snickered, and her stodgy professor glared from his place at the front of the room.

"Are we boring you, Mrs. Price?" he asked shortly.

Remi ran her hand across her eyes, trying to rub away the

CHAPTER TWELVE

remnants of sleep. "No, sir." She couldn't believe she'd fallen asleep in class. She'd never done that. Not even as a child.

"Then perhaps you are ill. Maybe you should leave class to not infect the rest of us."

Remi looked at the professor with disbelief.

"Now, Mrs. Price. And perhaps your friend should go with you."

Remi gave Sophia a sympathetic smile and the two girls quickly gathered their things before leaving the classroom.

"What the hell is wrong with you?" Sophia hissed as soon as the door to the classroom snapped shut behind them. She grabbed Remi's arm and dragged her down the hall to a bathroom and forced her friend to look in the mirror.

Remi was pale, there were dark circles under her eyes, her eye makeup was smudged all over her face, and her cheeks were sunken in. She hadn't looked this bad since her first night at Blackwood Manor, when Richard's aunt Claire attacked her in an attempt to force them out of the house.

"Are you still not sleeping? Don't you dare lie to me."

Remi told Sophia everything and watched her face change from a look of concern, to one of horror.

"Run," Sophia said simply once she was done.

"Sophia, I can't go anywhere." Remi leaned over the basin to splash cool water on her face.

"Remi, what did we say a few days ago? Once things moved from dreams to reality you'd run. It's escalated so much quicker than we thought."

"I can't run, okay? I have a husband, I have two kids, and I have a business. It's not quite that simple."

They both jumped when a stall opened behind them and a long-legged blonde stepped out. Violet Davis. She was a snobby, plastic doll-looking type, who was always looking down on everyone around her. No one liked her, but many put up with her because she had money.

"You know," Violet walked up to the sink beside Remi and examined her make-up in the mirror, "you're smarter than this, Remi. You can't be surprised when something like this happens at Blackwood Manor."

"Fuck off, Violet," Sophia said before placing a hand on Remi's shoulder and attempting to shift her position so her back was to Violet.

"It's true," Violet laughed, and walked back around so she could look into Remi's face again, with a hand on her hip. "You need to look out for yourself. And your kids. Don't let that man drag you down. He's an idiot for buying the place. You three don't have to pay the price."

"He didn't buy the place, you stupid bimbo." Sophia's nose flared as she spoke. "He inherited it."

Violet shrugged. "Big diff. He's still an idiot for having his family there knowing what it is. He can't sell it because of what it is. They would be better off leaving it to rot."

"Nothing's happened in three years," Remi whispered with a cracking voice.

Violet snorted. "Honey. Things can lay dormant for years. Doesn't mean they're any less dangerous. I don't see why that place would be any different."

"Get the hell out of here. Talking about things you know nothing about," Sophia said again.

Violet ignored Sophia. She looked deeply into Remi's eyes. "We're talking about your kids here. Not your husband. Not you. Your kids. Think about that."

With that statement, Violet flung her hair over her shoulder and strode out of the room.

"God, I hate it when she's right," Sophia said under her breath once the door closed.

Remi pulled makeup wipes out of her purse and began to remove her smudged eye make-up. "Did I say anything when I was asleep? Everyone was staring."

Sophia shook her head. "No. But you were groaning, and your body went kind of rigid. You kinda looked like you were convulsing."

Great. She was going to be the laughing stock of the school now.

Sophia must have known what she was thinking, because she put a comforting hand on Remi's shoulder. "Hey, don't worry about it. We've all had our share of sleepless nights. It's med school. They'll understand."

Remi put her back to the sink and shook her head. "No, it's more than that. I can't stop thinking about what my mom said about Kylie. Her eyes—"

"Maybe she was screwing with you," Sophia said gently.

Remi shook her head again. "No. My mom's not the joking type. Besides, she doesn't know about the house."

"All it would take is a quick internet search."

Remi hadn't thought about that. Had her parents researched Blackwood Manor before coming?

"Alright," Sophia patted her back. "You need sleep. I'm taking you home, and you're going straight to bed. I don't want to hear any arguments."

"But the girls—"

"I will take the girls to the park." Sophia smiled. "I got you, chick."

***

When they arrived back at Blackwood Manor, Natalie stood in the parlor with the strangest looking woman Remi had ever seen.

The woman stood in long, flowy, multicolored skirts, a fitted, corset-like top, and her gray hair flowed freely past her waist. Hoop earrings hung from her ears, and one word came to mind. Psychic. This was a stereotypical image she'd remembered seeing on television as a child.

"Remi!" Natalie called out and gestured for her to come forward. "This is Nadine Lewis. She read my email and came to see us."

Sophia put her hands on Remi's shoulders and steered her toward the staircase. "This will have to wait. Remi needs sleep."

Natalie narrowed her eyes at Sophia, but she didn't object. Remi allowed herself to be led upstairs and into the family wing. She was promptly deposited onto the air mattress and Sophia left the room without another word.

Remi turned to her side and closed her eyes. She was asleep before she could finish pulling the bedspread up.

A blue fog filled her vision. She flew through the air as if she were riding a runaway roller coaster. Images of her life swirled around her in the fog.

"No! No! No!" Malaki screamed at her. Her nine-year-old self put her violin down as the tears rolled down her cheeks. "That's the wrong chord! How many times do we have to go over this!"

CHAPTER TWELVE

"You would be so pretty if you lost about ten pounds," Mira said from her other side as she patted her thirteen-year-old tummy. "How can you expect to catch a husband if you're tubby?"

Then she started seeing flashes of someone else's life. A tall woman wearing a black mourning dress, knelt on the ground outside the cellar door, cradling a blonde child, who was lying in a pool of blood. The woman cried inconsolably while another woman looked on in horror, with a hand to her mouth. "Miss Margaret! What did you do?"

Another flash of that same woman peeking around the corner of the parlor at the back of a small blonde child humming and pulling the head off a doll.

Remi was catapulted forward, and spun through the air, before slamming to a stop suspended upside down.

"My, my. Aren't you a pretty one?" A woman came into focus. She was impossibly beautiful. Her raven black hair hung in shiny, soft waves, framing porcelain-like skin.

The woman wore a dress of soft pink, made from the finest silk. She came to a stop when she and Remi were eye to eye.

"Who are you?" Remi asked softly.

"Rebecca."

Remi narrowed her eyes. "You're the witch who cursed my land."

Rebecca laughed. "First off, my dear, it is my land. It always has been. It always will be. Why would I curse my own land?"

"Out of anger. The land got split and this house was built. You were angry over losing a parcel."

"That was well after my time."

"Yes, but it was your descendants. Acting under your authority."

Rebecca snorted. "My descendants? I have seen inside your soul, Remi Huang Price. Tell me, how should I be held responsible for the actions of my descendants, long after my demise? Are you responsible for the actions of your parents? Is your husband? Bloodline does not automatically equate culpability."

Remi ignored the question. She would not talk about the strained relationship with her family. Especially not with this woman who caused so much heartache.

"Why are you here?" she asked through clenched teeth. "We lifted your curse three years ago with the haven stone. You shouldn't be here."

"Again," Rebecca's tone was clipped. "It was not my curse. And you didn't lift anything."

"Bullshit!" Remi exclaimed. "The haven stone was made by a good witch to combat evil. It opened the door to the other side and allowed the spirits in the house to assist us. After it was done, they all crossed over."

Rebecca sighed. "Humans are so dense. *I* created the haven stone. *Because* of the curse."

"You did? Why?"

"Because I was appalled by what I saw those people doing on my land! Yes, I had magic, but I never used it for such torrid purposes. I happen to love children. Sacrificing them? And for what? A *harvest*? But my body had long since been in the earth. The stone was my best chance of restoring the balance."

"But we found the stone," Remi protested. "It did do something. You're saying we didn't restore the balance?"

Rebecca shook her head. "Close. You did clear a lot of energy. Opened the doorway so many of the innocent could leave. The ones that were trapped against their will. But others remain.

CHAPTER TWELVE

Some are merely stubborn; others have ill intent. But the bones of the curse remain, waiting."

"Why didn't it work?"

"The stone was in the hands of the right bloodline, but the wrong person. The intended had not been born yet."

Remi forced down the lump in her throat. "And they still haven't been born?"

"She has," Rebecca inclined her head.

No. No. A sweat instantly broke out over Remi's body. Had not been born then. Is now born. This woman, this witch, was talking about either Emily or Kylie.

"I need you to listen to me very closely," Rebecca leaned closer. "She will not come into her power for several years yet. That doesn't mean that the curse won't try to dig its heels in before then. It will try to dispose of her by any means possible. You mustn't let it in. Protect her at all costs. Then when the time comes, she will need to use the haven stone. That's very important."

"We can move away," Remi whispered. She hated to utter the words aloud. She'd grown to love Blackwood Manor. She loved the life they'd built here.

"It wouldn't do any good. She would end up coming back later. They always do. And she won't have your protection if that happens."

"Well, I'm not going to raise my children to be soldiers for a ghost war, no offense. We'll ignore it."

"Don't be a fool. You sound like that other one. Look at how it worked out for her."

"Who?"

"I don't know," Rebecca sighed. "Names and faces tend to blur together over time. There was another who was meant to break the curse. But her mother didn't heed my warnings."

"Think hard. What was her name? Is she still there?"

Rebecca didn't answer, and Remi was once again enveloped in the swirling blue fog.

CHAPTER THIRTEEN

Remi

Remi's mind didn't have time to clear before she slammed back into her body.

"Remi. What are you doing? What are you *doing?*" a voice yelled at her.

She opened her eyes and was astonished to see she was on her knees. There was heaviness in her arms, and she looked down at Kylie, who was cradled in her arms. The baby screamed and waved her tiny arms. Kylie's eyes were black as night. Remi nearly dropped her from the shock, but a pair of strong arms reached out and snatched the baby away before she could drop her.

"What the hell is wrong with you?" Richard snarled before rushing from the room with Kylie.

"Remi? What's going on?" Natalie was there. She knelt to the ground to be eye level with Remi. That's when she realized where she was. She was seated on the floor of the bathroom. Her hair hung in her face in soaking wet ropes. The bathtub was filled to the brim with water. It had overrun a bit, and water was puddled under her.

"Remi!" Natalie said again, more insistently this time. Remi's eyes snapped back to her friend's face. She tried to respond, but she couldn't. Her arms trembled, and her breathing turned harsh.

"Breathe," Natalie said. She put a hand on each side of Remi's face and took a slow, deliberate breath in, then let it out. "Breathe," she said again softly, and repeated the exercise.

Remi followed her lead, and her breathing evened, and her heart rate slowed. She was still confused and scared.

"What happened?" she finally asked.

Natalie dropped her hands to her lap. "We came looking for you and found you in here. You were leaning in front of the tub with Kylie."

"Kylie. Oh my God, is she okay?"

Natalie nodded. "You look like you went for a dip and then went to retrieve her."

"I don't understand. The girls shouldn't even be here. Sophia was taking them to the park."

Natalie's eyes filled with concern. "Remi, she did. That was yesterday."

"No. It's only been a few minutes."

Natalie shook her head. "No. Sophia brought you home to get some sleep because you fell asleep in class. She took the girls to the park so you could get some rest. You were still asleep when she brought them home a couple of hours later. We all knew how exhausted you've been, so we decided to let you sleep. We came to get you for breakfast, and you're—" she gestured toward the sorry state that Remi was in. "Do you remember anything at all?"

"I remember coming home with Sophia and laying down."

"Did you have one of your nightmares? Think hard. When

CHAPTER THIRTEEN

I touched you, something was there but there was a black veil over it, blocking it."

Remi squeezed her eyes closed and willed herself to remember. There was nothing for a moment, and then the conversation with Rebecca flashed through her mind like a movie on a projector. Her mouth dropped, and she stared at Natalie. Surely, that was only a dream. Please, let that have only been a dream.

Natalie tentatively lifted her hands once again and cupped Remi's face. She closed her eyes for a moment, then opened them again. She stared at Remi. "Oh my God."

"It was a dream, wasn't it?"

Natalie shook her head. "No. No. I don't think it was."

"So, what does this mean? One of the girls is the golden warrior? I thought that was Richard. That's how we were able to accomplish so much three years ago."

Natalie bit her lip. "He is the golden warrior. This goes deeper than that."

"How?"

"Well, I'm not an expert. This is out of the line of what I normally deal with. But I'm pretty sure she's saying that it can only be put to rest by a witch."

Remi stared at her dubiously. "And one of my girls is a witch?"

Natalie nodded. "Not only that. It seems like almost this exact situation has happened before."

"When?"

"Let's say, I think we're starting to get an inside look into what was going through Margaret Blackwood's head back in the day."

* * *

Remi sat on the front steps with her forehead resting on her knees. She didn't know how to process everything that was happening. She'd very nearly done something unforgivable to her baby, and she hadn't even known it. Was this what happened to Margaret Blackwood? It was certainly Natalie's theory, and Natalie's gift was reliable. It was a pretty safe bet that she wasn't too far off.

Remi was terrified, and she didn't know how to handle it. She couldn't go down the same path as Margaret. It was inconceivable. Should she run away for the girls' own safety?

"Don't be so dense," Rebecca's voice thundered in her head, causing Remi to squeal and jump. *"All that would do is remove your protection."*

Remi sobbed. That was the second time Rebecca said that, but she didn't understand what the witch wanted from her. How was she supposed to protect her children if she was ultimately the one destined to bring them harm?

"Mrs. Price?" a voice jerked her from her thoughts.

Remi raised her tear-streaked face to see the woman Natalie talked to in the parlor. "Yes?"

"I'm Nadine Lewis," the woman said pleasantly and held out her hand. The gesture puzzled Remi. It was as if she were introducing herself after bumping into each other at the grocery store, not as if she were staring at a hysterical, soaking wet woman who tried to kill her child.

Remi didn't respond, but she took the other woman's hand anyway.

CHAPTER THIRTEEN

"Natalie called me," Nadine said. "She asked me to come out and talk to you. Maybe we should find a less conspicuous place to talk." She nodded toward the window behind her, and Remi followed her gaze.

The puzzled faces of several guests glanced out the dining room window. Great. She hadn't even thought about how she was parading around what happened this morning by being out here.

Remi nodded and got to her feet. She led Nadine around the corner of the house and out to the cottage at the back of the grounds.

The cottage had once been servant's quarters in the days of the Civil War, then years later, it served as the home of Richard's little family because his mother hadn't wanted to live in the main house. She didn't trust it. Turns out she'd been right to fear it, but the precaution did nothing in the end.

Remi took a seat on the couch and pulled her knees to her chest. Nadine sat in a chair next to her and gave her a sympathetic look. "This must be a lot to take in."

Remi wiped a tear away and finally looked into Nadine's eyes. "Did Natalie tell you what happened?"

Nadine inclined her head. "She did."

Remi sighed shakily and trembled.

"It isn't your fault. You didn't know what you were doing," the other woman said gently and reached over to take her hand.

"Yes, it is." Remi shook her head. She couldn't stop thinking about the horrific sight in front of her when she'd come back to herself. In a weird way, she was grateful it hadn't been Emily. Kylie wouldn't remember this. Richard would, though. Richard would never forget it. Remi saw the look on his face when he found them in front of the bathtub, and it was nothing but pure hate.

"You're not yourself during possession."

Is that what happened? Remi never even thought about it. Her experience seemed different than the cases of possessions that she knew about. Jessie, for example, told her it felt like she was a prisoner in her own body, she could hear the thoughts of another person, see their actions, but could do nothing to stop them. Sometimes it was there, sometimes it wasn't.

Remi told Nadine this. "It doesn't sound like possession to me."

"It was," Nadine told her confidently. "The manifestation can differ based on a number of factors. The intention of the possessor versus the mental state and strength of the possessee. It sounds to me that your friend had leeway because she was being possessed by a friend. She got a break every now and again."

Remi scoffed. She doubted Jessie would describe any part of her experience as, "having a break." She hadn't known what reality was half the time.

As if reading her mind, Nadine continued. "Not to discredit what she went through, of course. I'm saying her friend didn't completely take over her mind, and when she used her body, it was to try to get help for the situation. She didn't realize the damage she was causing. The intentions were pure."

That explanation made slightly more sense to Remi, but she still didn't like it. "You, however, have a very strong spirit. If I'm not mistaken, you may be a bit touched yourself." Nadine winked at her. "You wouldn't be easily manipulated, so the spirit that possessed you needed to lull you into a dream state in order to do what it wanted."

CHAPTER THIRTEEN

"So, you've seen this before?" Remi's voice swelled with hope, and she turned to better face her visitor. "What do we do about it?"

Nadine's smile was half-hearted. "I see spirits, and sometimes I see demons too. But I'm no expert on how to deal with them. I can't banish them or change the trajectory of time. I can merely tell you what I'm seeing to hopefully better prepare you."

Remi told Nadine about the battle three years ago with the neighboring estate, how they'd banded together with many spirits, and how so many were obliterated. She told her they'd had no activity in the time in between, about seeing Lucy in the doorway to the nursery, and how they'd thought she was one of the banished spirits.

"Yes, Lucy is still here," Nadine confirmed and nodded her head. "When I visited the property thirteen years ago, I detected well over three hundred spirits. Most are gone. Between the family that was here at the time, and whatever you all did three years ago, many got cleared. There are still spirits here, however. I detected around twenty. There could have been a couple more hiding. Not too many more. I would have felt it. While there are not as many spirits remaining, there are still a handful that are relatively bitter. You need to be aware and mindful of that."

"So, if Lucy is still here, I'm assuming Margaret is too?" That made the most sense to Remi. Margaret had to be trying to get inside her mind.

"Margaret?"

"Oh wow." Remi tried to think of the best way to tell Nadine who she meant. "I never saw her in person, but I saw a video she was in. Tall woman, horns on her head, blue skin? She would have been wearing floor length skirts from the Civil War era. She's Lucy's mother?"

Nadine shook her head. "No. I didn't see anyone fitting that description inside. If she was there, she was hiding from me."

Remi bit her lip. She doubted Margaret *could* hide. Even if she wanted to. It was her understanding that the woman had a magnetic presence. If Nadine couldn't sense her, maybe she *wasn't* there. But if that were the case, why was she experiencing the woman's twisted thoughts as surely as if they were one.

"I did get the vibes from a few of the spirits that they were unhappy—even bitter. Two of them felt particularly dark. I don't know their names, so please don't ask. One is a woman. She radiates hate. It nearly took my breath away. Her features are also not visible. She is encased almost entirely in shadow."

"Then it could be Margaret?"

"No. This spirit is small in stature. I could almost mistake it for a child but—"

"But?"

"But the energy is different. It's really hard to explain. Ask Natalie. She may be able to articulate it better than me. It's the type of thing you can't really understand unless you have a gift with the other side."

Maybe she could understand. She wasn't sure if what she had was a gift, but *something* was going on. She'd even been on the other side of the veil before and had a full-on conversation with Josie. Of course, she'd been unconscious at the time. But the information she'd gotten during that conversation was useful.

"What about the other one?"

"It's a man. He wore a Union uniform and had a handlebar

mustache. He struck me as lewd, and my skin crawled in his presence."

Remi cocked her head to the side. She vaguely recalled a soldier being mentioned way back in the day, but he hadn't been given too much attention.

"So, what do you think I should do?"

"I wish I could tell you," Nadine attempted to smile, but it came out forced. "This is out of my area of expertise."

"Should I leave the house?"

"That won't do anything, you imbecile!" the voice thundered in her head again.

"I doubt it would help. You've been targeted for a reason. You may very well be left alone but those that remain will be more vulnerable. Also, I think it's fair to say if you're meant to be here, you'll be pulled back eventually. There's a force around Blackwood Manor. It's like a disgusting horror movie scene that twists your stomach, but you can't look away."

Remi nodded. She didn't know what to make of this new information. Sure, she knew more now than she did before, but what good would that do if she couldn't use it to her advantage?

"My dear," Nadine took her hand and held it firmly, "all is not lost."

"How did you know—"

Remi was cut off when she looked into Nadine's eyes. They were rolled back in her head revealing the whites. Remi's blood ran cold, and she tried to shake her hand from the woman's grasp, but she held tightly.

"You have tools at your disposal. You only need to think hard."

"What are you doing?" a voice thundered from across the

room.

Remi squealed and jerked back to look at who spoke.

Fire radiated through Remi's body from trying to jerk away while Nadine clung to her arm. A man materialized from the shadows leading into the hallway. He had thinning red hair, a paunchy gut, and hard beady eyes. Horns sat atop his head. His skin wasn't scaly, but it had the slightest blue tint. "We don't interfere!"

"Oh, really?" Nadine chuckled and stared at him with those blank eyes. "Mr. Vodka?"

The man screamed in rage and ran at Nadine in a full tackle. The chair she was in toppled over, flinging the woman backward.

"Stop it! Stop that!" Remi screamed.

Just like that the man was gone.

Nadine sat up and rubbed her neck. Her eyes were back to normal. "Oh my. That hasn't happened in a while."

CHAPTER FOURTEEN

Margaret

Margaret's peace after locking the girl in the cellar was short-lived. She'd found Josie sneaking out of the cellar with an empty food tray the night before. She was beginning to think Josie was another problem she'd need to navigate.

She wished she could say she was surprised that Josie was sneaking the girl food, despite being explicitly told not to, but she wasn't.

The frequency with which she stood up for the girl's indiscretions was maddening. Worse, was how comfortable she was with questioning her parenting decisions. Yes, Josie would need to be dealt with soon.

It was a shame because Margaret loved Josie. She knew the other woman didn't currently believe it, but it was true. She'd watched Josie blossom, and she was such a kind and compassionate person. Margaret considered Josie her best friend, despite the relationship being looked down on by high society and her own in-laws. She knew her own father would skin her hide if he caught wind of how friendly she was with

Josie. Luckily, when she'd married John, that part of her life was severed.

Still, the other woman was too comfortable. Her fondness made her too lenient. Guilt flooded her as she massaged her hand, which still stung from when she'd slapped Josie the night before. She'd never hit anyone before in her life, never even thought of it. But something inside of her unraveled, and she hadn't thought about what she was doing.

"She's your daughter," Josie's words echoed in her mind. That *thing* was not her daughter! Why couldn't she get anyone to understand that? Even the children were treating her differently now. Lucy actually rolled her eyes at her last week. She was way too young to be exhibiting that kind of behavior. It was Josie and that blasted demon in the cellar turning them against her.

Weeks passed since Margaret told Josie to ask about anyone willing to discreetly take the girl to the orphanage and save them all this heartache. She either hadn't done as she was told, or she hadn't been able to find anyone. Margaret didn't know. They hadn't discussed it since. Her blood boiled every time she thought of the insinuation they put Lucy in an institution. Margaret read about those places. They weren't humane. Imagine. Her baby in a place like that! She silently admitted to herself that the slap had partially been over the audacity.

Margaret descended the stairs and followed the sounds of her children into the dining room. When she entered the room, Lucy and Percy stopped talking and looked at their plates like they were the most interesting things in the world. Josie entered from the kitchen with a pitcher of milk. She hesitated when she saw Margaret, then moved to pour the children's glasses.

CHAPTER FOURTEEN

Margaret cleared her throat. "Josie, I wanted to apologize again for what happened last night. We do need to discuss your conduct, but I never should have struck you."

Margaret caught Percy and Lucy exchanging a look across the table. "What?" she snapped at them.

"Nothing, Mama," Percy said as he picked up his glass of milk.

"It most certainly is not nothing. Out with it. If you have something to say, you say it. We don't keep secrets in this house."

"Don't we?"

The words were so shocking that Margaret felt as if she'd been run over by a wagon. She sunk into her seat at the table but did not take her eyes off her son. "Excuse me?"

"Well, Gloria's a secret, isn't she? We're not even supposed to talk about her with each other. Will anyone else ever know? Will father?"

"Who the devil is Gloria?"

Percy and Lucy exchanged another glance over the table, but neither of them answered her.

Margaret brought her gaze back to Josie. "You named her?" she asked through clenched teeth. Her hand trembled, aching to reach over and slam into the woman, but she forced herself to leave it on the table.

Josie flushed, but she didn't meet her gaze. "We couldn't keep calling her 'it' or 'her', Miss Margaret. It was getting confusing."

"Alright." It took everything within her to keep Margaret from screaming at the top of her lungs. She fought to keep her voice calm and even as she looked back at Percy. "I stand corrected. We do have a secret. A secret that is between the four of us in this room. It won't go outside the house. But we can't keep secrets from each other. That's when everything will crumble. You shouldn't keep secrets from your mother. So, tell me. What was that look between the two of you?"

Lucy's breath shook but it was Percy who answered her. "Well, it's just that you hit Josie, and she's supposed to be your best friend. You're so angry all the time. You don't even look like yourself."

Fury bubbled in her stomach, but she couldn't very well punish the boy. He spoke the truth. She'd hit Josie. She was angry and snapped at them a lot. She couldn't even deny she looked different now. She'd been steadily losing weight, and her cheeks were now all sharp lines and sunken.

"Alright," she said again. What else was there to say? Everyone was against her.

"Then the way you are with Gloria—" he broke off and looked at a spot on the wall, as if trying to think of the best way to form his words. "Well, we can't help but wonder. What if we're next?"

"Oh, for the love of—" Margaret forced herself to bite off the hateful phrase before it could leave her lips. "She's the devil!"

"No, Mama. She's a little girl. Like me." Lucy's voice shook and tears filled her eyes. It was that sight that broke Margaret.

"You poor, innocent child," Margaret leaned over and reached out her arms to embrace Lucy, but the child pulled away as if her touch would burn. "Can't you see that's what she wants? She wants you to think I'm mistreating her. To tear us apart."

"We're not blind, Mama," Percy said harshly. His voice held a firmness that was far beyond his years, and his eyes were cold. "We know you mistreat her. You mistreat all of us. Something

CHAPTER FOURTEEN

has to change around here. We want our mama back or we want to leave."

"Well, that's too bad, isn't it?" she retorted, her patience gone. "I'm the mother and I make the rules. I swear everyone here has become beyond spoiled and that's what's going to change."

"There are things that can be done about it," he said with a low voice. "When we went into town Thursday I snuck away and went to enlist, but they said I was too young."

This kept getting worse! Of course, they said he was too young! He was only nine years old!

Margaret glared at Josie once again. "You lost one of my children in town?"

"He was supposed to be hitching the team." Josie whispered in a soft voice.

"Don't blame her. She didn't know what I was doing," Percy snapped. For all his reluctance to speak up in the beginning, he certainly wasn't holding back now. "You know, I've been reading law books. You aren't untouchable. There are places the criminally insane can be sent. I'd say a secret daughter in the cellar qualifies, wouldn't you?"

Without thinking, Margaret grabbed Lucy's cup of milk from the table and threw it in his face.

Percy didn't flinch. He merely took the back of his hand and wiped the offending fluid away from his eyes.

Lucy let out a squeal of fright, and Josie hissed, "Miss Margaret!" in shock.

Margaret ignored the two of them, instead keeping her focus on her son. "Go to your room," she said through clenched teeth.

He didn't move at first, prompting her to scream, "NOW!"

She didn't recognize the inflection of her own voice when she gave the order, or the one in her voice when she looked at Josie as Percy scurried from the room.

"And you. Get out of my sight."

"Miss Margaret—"

"I'm extremely close to ordering you from the house, not my sight. Do not test me."

Josie inclined her head and disappeared through the door to the kitchen.

Margaret returned her attention to Lucy who sat next to her with a beet red, tear-streaked face, and softened her voice.

"Lucy, honey. She's not a normal little girl like you. She tells you to do horrible things."

"No, she doesn't," Lucy protested.

"She does. Please, don't lie for her."

"She doesn't!" Lucy insisted. "The girl does!"

"She is the girl."

"No, she's not!" Lucy brought down a fist on the table. "The girl was here before Gloria was ever born. She's always been here! It's the girl who lives in my closet!" Lucy's voice broke on her sobs. "Oh, never mind. You never believe me anyway."

Before Margaret could respond, Lucy tossed her napkin on the table and fled the room crying.

CHAPTER FIFTEEN

Remi

When Remi woke up, there were tears staining her face. This was getting to be a very depressing habit. She opened her eyes, and the living room of the cottage came into focus.

"Well, you look nice and rested." Remi looked over to see Richard sitting in the chair Nadine was in earlier. She quickly sat up to face him. He wasn't wrong. Despite the tears, she did feel well rested. For the first time in a week, she felt like she'd actually slept.

She couldn't say the same for her husband. Richard had dark circles under his eyes, and he was disheveled. His eyes were red and puffy as if he'd been crying too. But she suspected he'd been crying for a different reason. Her shoulder twinged when she adjusted her position. She noticed a half-melted ice pack on the cushion next to her and realized she must have been out here a while.

"What time is it?" she asked.

Richard shrugged. "I don't know. I think it's been the longest day of my life."

"Is Kylie okay?"

"No thanks to you."

His words stung more than she cared to admit, even though they were entirely justified. "Richard," she said weakly, "I wasn't in my right mind. I would never hurt the girls willingly."

Richard sighed and ran a hand through his hair. "I know. Natalie told me about the dream, or trance, or whatever it was. But Remi, I'm scared. We can't keep doing this. If I walked in that door a minute later—"

"I know," she said softly. "I'm terrified too."

"So, this is what I think we should do," he said and leaned forward to rest his arms on his knees. "I think you should go to a motel. Just until we get all this settled down and have a game plan."

Remi shook her head. "I thought about that, but I don't think it'll make a difference."

"Why is that?"

"How much did Natalie tell you?"

"Only that you'd been deeply engrossed in a vision and had no clue what you were doing."

Remi launched into detail of her dream and talking to Rebecca. When she finished, his eyebrows were furrowed with confusion.

"So, we cleared a lot of negative energy, but we didn't break the curse? And one of our girls is supposed to be the one to do it?"

"That's what I got out of it," Remi nodded. "That's not even the most infuriating part. Every time I think about leaving for their safety, she tells me it wouldn't do any good."

"She's talking to you now? When you're awake?"

"Yes, but only if I think about leaving. I can't figure out what

CHAPTER FIFTEEN

I'm supposed to do. Nadine Lewis also told me that leaving wouldn't help. In fact, she implied it could make things worse."

"Nadine Lewis was here?" Richard seemed surprised. "Natalie said she was calling her, but I never saw her. "

"She ran into me on the porch. That's why I'm out here. We came in here to talk."

Remi brought him up to date on her conversation with Nadine.

"We're down to twenty? That's impressive."

"That's twenty more than we thought we had."

"Still, when you consider where we started that's pretty damn good."

"The good news is she only picked up on two negative spirits. I'm willing to bet it's one of them that's responsible for everything starting back up again."

Richard nodded in agreement. "Probably this shadowed woman, considering it's you."

"I do have questions about that soldier. He was here before, right? I seem to recall someone mentioning a soldier before, but he never seemed to be a major focus."

Richard nodded. "I never saw him, but I remember my family talking about it when I was a kid. They believed he was Gloria's father. Considering Josie's diary stated Gloria was the product of a rape by soldiers, it seems like a pretty safe bet. He's probably the one who tried to stop Nadine from warning you."

Remi shook her head. "No, it couldn't be him. Nadine said the soldier had a handlebar mustache and was in uniform. This man was sharply dressed, but he was more modernly dressed and there was no mustache."

Richard threw up his hands. "Well, that contradicts what she said already. She said there were only two negative spirits and one of them was the soldier. This man you saw was violent."

"I don't think he was. He didn't do anything to me. He wanted to stop her from telling me what to do. He left when she was down."

Richard gestured to her arm. "You did get hurt."

"That was from Nadine holding on so tight when she was in her trance. It wasn't intentional. I'm fine. Just a little sore."

He sighed again and bit his lip, deep in thought. "Okay, so you can't leave. That leaves the girls vulnerable. How about we see about getting you in to see a doctor under the guise of sleepwalking? And then you stay out here in the meantime?"

Remi couldn't help but chuckle. How ironic it was that she made up a half-assed sleepwalking excuse a few days ago, and now she would need to see a doctor for that very issue. "It's not technically sleepwalking, but maybe they'll have some ideas of what to do."

"You're going to say it's sleepwalking, though," Richard clarified. "What else are you going to say? An ancient witch who cursed my land told me an evil presence in my house is trying to get me to kill my kids? They'll lock you up."

Remi sighed. She didn't like lying, but she knew he was right. "How big of a complication are my parents posing?" It crossed her mind she'd been largely out of it the last couple of days. There was no way they hadn't noticed.

"Your dad has been gone a lot. So far, we've been able to pass it off as being opposite schedules. That won't last long. I think your mom knows something's going on we aren't sharing. Something about the looks she gives me. Luckily, she hasn't started asking questions yet."

"If she does, refer her to me. I'll take care of it."

CHAPTER FIFTEEN

"What will you say to her?"

"I don't know yet, but I'll figure it out. She's easier to handle than my father."

CHAPTER SIXTEEN

Remi

Remi didn't know how he did it, but Richard managed to get her an appointment for the following day. Normally, their primary care provider was booked three weeks out. She slugged through her class, then went straight to the doctor's office.

The receptionist, a sweet and bubbly woman by the name of Susan, waved and signed her in. She was taken back almost immediately.

When Doctor Taylor entered the room, he gave her a bright smile. He was a short, balding man with a pot belly and wore round, gold-rimmed glasses. Remi imagined that he was exactly what Santa Clause would look like without a beard. "Hello, Remi," he said as he took his seat. He glanced down at the chart in front of him before returning his gaze to her. "It looks like you're here today for sleepwalking?"

Remi nodded. "I haven't been sleeping the best lately. My husband found me before I stumbled down the stairs in our house the night before last." The story they'd rehearsed religiously rolled off her tongue. She almost believed herself.

CHAPTER SIXTEEN

"I didn't see a history of sleepwalking in your chart."

"No. I don't have a history of it. At least, I don't think so. No one's ever mentioned it to me, but obviously, that situation scared both me and my husband."

"You're in medical school, aren't you?"

"Yes."

"And I see you had your baby." His eyes twinkled.

"I did. Kylie just turned six weeks old." Yesterday. It was too bad that the milestone was overshadowed by everything that was going on at home.

Doctor Taylor nodded. "I can understand your concern, but I hope I can ease your fears. While sleepwalking is often attributed to an underlying medical condition, it can be completely situational. I believe that's the case here. Your lack of medical history, the demands of medical school, and caring for two small children, one of whom is a newborn, all point to it being situational. Your body's sleep rhythm has been thrown out of whack, and we need to get it back on track."

"Okay, so what do we do?"

"Well, there are a few medications we can try. You can also try adjusting your sleep schedule. Go to sleep at the same time every night. Set an alarm for about fifteen minutes before you normally begin to sleepwalk, then go back to sleep. I would also like to recommend some sort of a noise system to alert others when you are sleepwalking. Bells on the ankles and doorknobs are often successful. You can also buy door alarms at the hardware store."

"That's great. I will do all those things."

"I would also like to schedule a follow-up in a week to check in and make sure everything is going smoothly." He turned to his computer and pulled up her preferred pharmacy to send in a prescription.

***

Remi's mood was lifted when she left the doctor's office. When she walked into the kitchen entrance at Blackwood Manor, it was dashed.

Malaki sat at the island and smirked at her over the top of a newspaper. The island and counters were littered with various items. Mira was at the stove furiously trying to finish cooking.

Jessie stood behind him with her arms folded across her chest. Her cheeks were bright red, and her lips were set in a tighter line than Remi could remember ever seeing.

"What's wrong?" she asked cautiously.

"I'm late getting dinner started for the guests," Jessie said. "But your father wasn't happy with the menu and told your mother to make him something. Now I can't access anything."

"Guys, can you pick this up in about half an hour please?" Remi asked nicely.

Malaki shook his head and smirked again. "Your mother is in mid-preparation. It won't hurt them to wait an hour."

"Oh, for God's sake," Remi spat. She slammed her books down on the island and strode forward, grabbing the handle of the nearest pan her mother was using. She carried it to the garbage can and dumped the contents inside.

Malaki shot from his seat. "Just what the hell do you think you're doing, lady? Your parents come first."

CHAPTER SIXTEEN

"This is a business," she said firmly. "You were aware of this when you chose to stay here. Go on, Jessie."

Jessie stood there for a moment, speechless, and then rushed forward to claim the stove while she still had the chance.

Remi turned back to her father. "We have a strict timetable. We do everything to keep it running smoothly. I already told you once that you may not roam and do as you please in my home. It is *my* home. Mine and Richard's, and we make the rules. If you do one more thing that disturbs our way of life, I'll have to ask you to leave."

Unable to think of a reply, Malaki glanced around the room and spotted her prescription lying on the island. He snatched it. "What's this?"

Remi went to grab it, but he held it out of her reach. "You're on drugs? That's why you're acting so erratic?"

"What the hell is going on in here?" Richard entered from the dining room. His hair stood up every which way, and he looked even more worn down than the last time Remi saw him. She had the passing thought that he might need to see a doctor too.

"Your wife is a dopehead," Malaki sneered and tossed the prescription to Richard, who caught it easily. "That's why she's been acting so crazy."

"It's for my sleepwalking," Remi told him gently. She was relieved to see the expression on his face. There was no question. No doubt. He believed her. Thank God.

"Sleepwalking?" Malaki hissed. "What a pathetic lie. You don't sleepwalk."

"Well, I've started recently," she shot back. "I went to the doctor after school today. He said stressful situations can bring it on. I wonder what could be going on in my life that's so stressful."

Richard tried to break the tension in the room by speaking to Jessie. "How much longer on dinner? The guests are getting antsy."

"I'm just starting, Richard. I'm so sorry."

"Just starting?"

"Yes, Richard," Remi said. "She's just starting because my father decided to act like a toddler and demand a different dinner than everyone else. These two took over the kitchen and wouldn't let her do her job. When I stopped the situation and dumped what they were preparing he decided to accuse me of doing drugs."

Richard turned his attention to Malaki. "Malaki, I'm sorry. She's right. I wish it hadn't needed to turn into such a blow up, but our guests expect their dinner at six o'clock. If you didn't like what was on the menu, you could have ordered something in or waited until we were done in the kitchen."

"Richard, son," Malaki said with a clipped voice, "I don't expect you to understand because you don't have a family. But *she* knows better." He jerked his head toward Remi. "Family always comes first. Especially parents."

Remi watched the fury fill Richard's eyes, and his jaw firmly set. *"Yes. Good. Get mad,"* she thought to herself. *"Be on my side."*

"You need to go."

"Excuse me?"

"You need to pack your things and go. You have disrespected my wife on multiple occasions and now you're making baseless accusations because you didn't get your way on dinner. You're jeopardizing our business, and her mental health. You're not welcome here anymore. You need to leave."

CHAPTER SIXTEEN

Remi's heart soared. Richard was never as attractive to her as he was at that moment.

"I'm not going anywhere."

"Oh, you're leaving one way or another," Richard said simply. "Don't make me have you removed. Mira can stay if she wants. She hasn't been disrespectful. But you have to go."

"Mira isn't staying anywhere I'm not welcome," he hissed before turning to his wife. "Come along."

"Mr. Price," Remi whispered. She glided toward him and slipped her arms around his neck. "So forceful."

Jessie let out a pointed cough to remind them she was still there.

Remi laughed, but she didn't pull away.

Richard grinned. "Do you feel better?"

"I do actually," she gave him a quick kiss.

"Good. What do you say we get out there and do damage control?"

She agreed and they headed toward the dining room hand in hand.

CHAPTER SEVENTEEN

Remi

That night, Remi collapsed next to Richard breathing heavily from their love making. It was the first time they'd been together since Kylie was born, and they'd desperately needed it.

"Damn, Remi," Richard panted. "I think you killed me."

She giggled, curled into the crook of his arm, and slid an arm across his chest. It was true. She'd been the one to take control. How could she not after the display downstairs? She loved seeing him one hundred percent in her corner. The devotion was the sexiest thing in the world to her.

She couldn't help but cling to him now. It felt right. There was plenty of room in the bed since they'd reclaimed their bedroom. It was nice to get off the air mattress, but she didn't want to let him go tonight.

"What did the doctor say?" Richard asked gently.

Remi was glad he did. She'd nearly nodded off in the afterglow of their lovemaking.

She quickly filled him in on her visit.

CHAPTER SEVENTEEN

"Well, I don't think waking you up before you start sleepwalking will help. It's so random and related to your dreams. Bells, though?"

Remi nodded. "I thought it was a good idea, so I grabbed a few from the discounted Christmas section at the thrift store on the way home."

"Show me?"

Remi groaned in protest, but she did roll off the bed and head over to the dresser where she'd set her shopping bags earlier. She pulled out a string of small bells.

Richard chewed his lip. "Do you think those will be loud enough to wake me up? Don't they make door alarms now? You know, that are motion activated."

Remi nodded. "The doctor suggested those too, and I did think about that, but they are crazy loud, and we have a business to run. We don't want to scare the shit out of the guests in the middle of the night. I figure we can start with these. If they don't work, we can reconsider the alarms."

"You're right," Richard picked up a string of bells and frowned. "I'm still not convinced this will wake me up."

"It's definitely a risk, but anything bigger will be too heavy. I thought you wanted me to stay in the cottage."

He squeezed her hand. "I don't think it's necessary if I can wake up in time to stop you from doing something. I don't want to be away from you." He brought her hand to his lips and kissed it.

Richard grabbed a length of string from the bag and walked over to the doorknob to their bedroom. He tied one of the lengths of bells from the knob and opened the door about a quarter of an inch. The bells gave a satisfying *ding* as they clanged together.

"So, what now? We tie the other one to you?"

Remi nodded and let him tie the bell to her wrist.

They looked at each other nervously and slid beneath the sheets.

CHAPTER EIGHTEEN

Margaret-1864

Margaret's hand trembled as she clenched the letter. Her throat was so dry she feared it may close. She'd read the letter many times, both loving and hating the words that filled the page.

John was coming home. He'd been injured, and he was coming home. It had been so long since she'd seen him, and she was thrilled that he was coming home. But there was one little problem. The girl. How would she explain her?

Margaret got up from the end of her bed and paced the floor, trying to think of what to do. She'd spent time trying to get the demon out of the girl. She'd figured John may be able to forgive her indiscretions if the girl was a pleasant child. But that hadn't happened, and time was running out.

Margaret took a deep breath and opened the drawer of her bedside table. She stared down at the gun that John left behind. She'd known it was here all along. One might question why she hadn't used it when the soldiers invaded her home. There were several answers to that. One thing was that they were outnumbered. She might have been able to take out one of them, but she would likely have been shot. There were the children to think of. Another reason was, she honestly thought she deserved it for being unfaithful to John.

She reached a shaking hand in the drawer and pulled it out. She'd never touched the thing before. But it couldn't be helped now.

Margaret set the gun down on the table and wiped her sweaty palm on her skirts before picking it back up. She thanked the heavens it was so late at night. Josie was safely asleep in the cottage out back. Margaret knew there was a good chance Josie would leave for good when she learned what happened, but it was a risk she would have to take.

She slowly made her way down the stairs and toward the door of the cellar. Pausing outside, she squeezed her eyes shut and counted to ten. Could she do this? Yes, the child was difficult. Yes, she didn't want her. But she was still a child.

The door to the cellar creaked open, and Margaret spotted a flash of blonde hair. Fury ignited inside her. Any doubts she had were squashed. This proved she was right. The demon did sneak out of the cellar at night and tell her children wicked things.

As this devil girl turned her back to close the cellar door, Margaret lifted her hand and fired the gun. It was surprisingly easy. The loud bang echoed off the walls of the otherwise silent house.

Her mouth dropped open as the girl gave a strangled cry and slowly turned. She was looking down at her chest where blood seeped and spread. Then she looked up at Margaret with eyes of horror.

Lucy? Margaret blinked several times, trying to will the scene before her to unfold differently, but it was no use. It

CHAPTER EIGHTEEN

was Lucy in front of her. Lucy who'd been sneaking out of the cellar. Lucy who she'd shot.

"Mama?" Lucy squeaked before collapsing to the ground.

Time stood still for Margaret. This couldn't be real. It was a dream in her head. She had them often. She subtly pinched her arm, but nothing changed. Lucy still lay lifelessly with blood flowing around her.

"Lucy," she finally said and craned her neck. Lucy didn't move. She was impossibly white.

"Move!" A voice thundered in her head. *"Do something!"*

"It won't do any good," another said. *"You killed her."*

Margaret lunged forward and pulled Lucy into her arms. "Lucy! Lucy, no!" she scolded sternly, but Lucy continued to lie there. Each passing second was agony.

"She's dead," the second voice taunted, but Margaret chose to ignore it. The alternative was unimaginable.

"Lucy, you stop fooling now!"

The front door burst open and slammed into the wall. Footsteps raced toward her, and she heard Josie's sharp intake of breath, but she couldn't look up from Lucy. She needed to see if she blinked or trembled.

"Miss Margaret?" Josie's voice had a strange, dreamlike quality about it, like they were underwater.

Josie knelt next to her, and her fingers closed around Lucy's tiny wrist. "Miss Margaret. She's gone."

Margaret's stomach dropped. Lucy wasn't playing a game. She didn't have a pulse and that could not be faked. Margaret allowed Josie to pull Lucy from her arms and tenderly close her eyes.

"What did you do?" Despite the question, Josie didn't seem accusatory. Her voice quavered, but it was sadness, not fear.

"She—she wasn't supposed to be down there."

"My God. What have I done?" Margaret thought to herself.

"You killed your daughter," the first voice scolded.

"She wasn't supposed to be where?" Josie asked.

"You killed your daughter," the first voice said again.

Before Margaret could answer Josie, the cellar door creaked open, and the girl's eye appeared in the crack.

"Lucy?" she called out.

The blood rushed in her ears as the voices hissed at her.

"It wasn't your fault," the second voice said. *"It was her. She made you do it. She tricked you."*

Margaret broke apart and reached out to roughly grab the girl.

"Miss Margaret, no!" Josie said.

Margaret ignored her, jerked the squirming child into her lap, and held her firmly. "Look. Look what you made me do!" she hissed into the child's ear.

The child wiggled and cried out, "No!" as she tried to break free.

"Let her go!" Josie demanded and grabbed hold of her shoulder.

Margaret loosened her grip on the girl to push Josie away, but it was enough. The child bit into Margaret's arm, hard, and slid out of her clutches.

"Little bitch!" Margaret howled. She jumped to her feet and went to sprint after the child, who ran up the stairs. She was tackled from behind and hit the floor. Josie tried to use her weight to pin her to the floor.

"Gloria, run!" Josie yelled at the girl.

"Let me go!" Margaret wailed. "She killed my baby! She killed my baby!"

CHAPTER EIGHTEEN

"She didn't! Miss Lucy was going down to the cellar every night for nearly a year to see her."

"No!" Margaret struggled against her.

"Yes! She wanted her sister!"

What was this? Margaret thought, desperately. Her precious daughter was lying dead mere feet away, and she wasn't being allowed to serve justice. It was wrong! It was sick and wrong!

Then it hit her. Josie always defended the girl. Josie loved the girl. Josie was trying to stop her from exorcising the demon, even as Lucy lay dead at their feet. She was in on it! She'd been in on it all along! How had she been so blind?

Ignited by the realization she'd been betrayed by her best friend, she brought an elbow into Josie's gut. The other woman gasped and rolled off her.

Margaret shot to her feet and ran to retrieve a fireplace poker. Josie grasped desperately at her skirts as she passed her on the way to the stairs. "She's the daughter of evil! She must be stopped!"

"Gloria, run!" Josie screamed again as she followed Margaret.

"The traitor is getting her second wind," Margaret thought to herself. *"I'll deal with her later."* She began to stick her head into various rooms.

"Come out, demon!" she yelled.

"Miss Margaret, please!" Josie pleaded as she grasped her sleeve. Margaret shook her off and headed down the hallway in the opposite direction. "See reason! What happened to Lucy is horrible, but it's not the girl's fault."

"Keep away from me!" Margaret shoved Josie with all her might. The woman lost her footing and tumbled over the banister.

Her shriek was the most horrible sound Margaret ever heard. There was a sickening smack as Josie hit the ground in the foyer.

Margaret nearly went to her but a voice in her head stopped her.

"There's nothing you can do for her now. Find the demon."

A cry down the hall brought her to the objective at hand. She branded the poker and followed the cries.

Margaret burst into Percy's bedroom. Her son knelt on the ground with his hands on the demon's shoulders, trying to calm her hysterical crying.

"Hide!" he was saying when the door opened. He jerked his head in her direction when the door opened.

"Mama," he said as he pulled the girl behind him in an attempt to block her body with his.

"Move, Percy," Margaret commanded.

"No, Mama," he shook his head.

Margaret snarled and grabbed his shirt, forcefully tossing him across the room. She then brought down the fireplace poker once, twice, three times until the only sound was Percy's sobs in the corner.

CHAPTER NINETEEN

Remi

Ding. Ding. The tingling of the bells woke Remi up as she crawled out of bed. Tears streamed down her face, and she felt as if she'd run a marathon. There was no question of what happened when she was asleep this time. Remi remembered every vicious detail as if she'd been there that night.

She sat back down on the edge of the bed and struggled to regain her breath. It was such a conflicting feeling. What Margaret did was horrible. No doubt about it. But she hadn't been in her right mind. If anyone could have benefited from an institution, it would have been Margaret Blackwood. She couldn't help but sympathize with her. One thing after another contributed to her mind breaking like a fragile piece of glass.

Remi turned to shake Richard awake and tell him what she'd seen but was startled to see that he wasn't in bed. She slipped on a robe and went to look for him. She checked Emily's room first. The girl had surprisingly gone to bed without any argument. Maybe it was finally getting her room back. Hopefully, they were at the end of that horrible stage.

She then checked the nursery. Kylie slept soundly and Remi quietly glided out of the room, making sure the baby monitor was in her robe pocket before heading downstairs.

Remi was shocked to find Richard standing silently in the darkness of the kitchen. He faced a certain cabinet that they had history with. Her breath caught in her throat, and she flicked on the light switch.

Richard swung around in surprise. There was a hard edge to his face, and his eyes were glazed over.

Remi was about to ask him if he was okay. Then it hit her. The smell. Liquor. Her heart dropped. He'd been doing so well for so long. She approached him to study his eyes. Then she remembered what the entranced Nadine Lewis called the man in the cottage before he'd tackled her. Mr. Vodka. Now the nickname made sense.

"You're drunk," she shook her head.

"No, I'm not, babe," he denied, but he stood awkwardly in front of the counter, and she knew what that meant.

Remi gently pushed him aside to reveal the half empty bottle of vodka sitting behind him. She picked it up and held it in front of his face.

"A guest must have left it," he shrugged.

"Don't you dare start lying to me," she snapped.

He hung his head in shame.

"How long has this been going on?"

Richard shrugged again. "About a week, I guess."

Remi slammed the bottle back down on the counter and walked to the kitchen table to sit. She was so damn mad. They'd worked so hard to get him sober.

She'd been understanding when it started. After they'd moved into Blackwood Manor years before, the bottle started appearing to Richard every time he opened that cabinet. Driven by the stress of what happened to his family, the shitty home life with his uncle growing up, and being back in the house, he'd indulged and gotten hooked.

Brad tried to get him to go cold turkey. Brad. That was a story for another day. He'd removed the offending bottle from the house. But the house learned, and started showing the bottle to only Richard, like a dirty little secret.

So, Natalie and Remi forbade him from setting foot in the kitchen for a while. It was a temporary fix, and they knew that. But they were up to their eyeballs in the investigation leading up to the battle and hadn't had time to do anything about it at the time.

After it was all said and done, Remi got him into AA and attended every single meeting with him. It wasn't pretty at first. He'd had terrible withdrawals, and she'd sat up with him during those long nights. He'd been doing well for so long.

She'd been worried he might be pushed over the edge when her parents showed up, but it turned out he'd been sneaking liquor since before then.

"You worked so hard," Remi said in disbelief. "*We* worked so hard."

"It's not that easy, Remi," he told her. "You've been to AA. You know that."

She did. But she also knew he hadn't been addicted nearly as long as some of the other people in those meetings, and he'd recovered relatively quickly. She'd hoped that the positive life they'd built together and their girls would be enough to deter him.

"Did you even try to not drink?"

"Yes, I did. I swear it." He sat opposite her at the table and took her hand. "I ignored it the first few times I saw it. Then it started appearing in other places. Bedroom closet, medicine cabinet. It was even in Emily's dresser once. I guess I figured if I didn't ignore it in the kitchen, it would stop appearing in other places. I was afraid Emily would get into it."

Remi sighed. "Okay. Well, we need to tell Natalie tomorrow. And you need to call your sponsor first thing in the morning. Do you still have his number?"

Richard nodded.

She should have pushed him to keep going to AA, but he'd seemed fine for so long. That was a mistake she wouldn't make again.

"Thanks, babe," Richard said and leaned in to kiss her head. She nearly pulled back from the smell on his breath, but she knew that wasn't what he needed right now. It was best to push through. "So, what did you come looking for me for?"

Remi told him about her dream of the night Lucy, Josie, and Gloria died. "I mean, we knew that's what happened, but it was so much worse than I could have ever imagined."

"You don't remember anything else?"

Remi shook her head. "There wasn't anything else. Why?"

"Well, there's something that's always bothered me. We know that the circular fireplaces were an addition put up to conceal Lucy's body. Margaret couldn't have done that by herself, and I seriously doubt Percy did it. He was what, nine? So, how did she manage to hide three murders and put up the false wall and fireplaces?"

Remi looked at him, stunned. She hadn't thought of that. It was such an obvious question, but it never once crossed her mind. It's not like there would have been a hardware store right down the street at that point in time. "I don't know," she admitted. "But it's hardly the only mystery around this house."

Richard laughed. "That's the damn truth."

They sat there in an awkward silence for a couple of minutes before Richard patted her hand. "I guess we better get to bed. We have a lot to go over with Natalie in the morning."

Remi nodded, but she was still deeply unsettled as they turned off the light and went upstairs.

CHAPTER TWENTY

Remi

"Why the hell didn't you call me?" Natalie crossed her arms in front of her and glared at Remi and Richard.

"It was the middle of the night," Remi said.

"That doesn't matter!" Natalie's eyes nearly bugged out of her head. "This is important. Both issues are important! If I'd come over here right away, I may have been able to pick up on residual energy. But no, there's nothing now."

They hung their heads like scolded children.

"We didn't think of it, Nat," Richard told her.

"Did it occur to either one of you that it's odd you both had these experiences at the same time? Something wanted to separate you."

Remi hadn't thought of it. She'd been dropping the ball a lot lately. She really needed to get her shit together. Her friend was right to be ripping her a new one. If the shoe were on the other foot, she'd do the same.

Richard seemed to have the same thought because he gave her a horrified look. What if she hadn't woken up when she did? What if she hadn't been able to snap him out of it before he was three sheets to the wind? Something did try to separate them. But why?

"Well, I think the first order of business is keeping your ass out of the kitchen," Natalie wagged a finger at Richard. "We might need to hire another person to make up the difference."

"He called his sponsor first thing this morning," Remi told her. She'd been the one to wake up early and hand him his cell phone. Then she stood over him while he'd hunted for the man's number and called him. She hated to admit it, but Brad would probably make a better sponsor for him.

They'd had a father/son bond back in the day before everything went sideways. Both of them suffering from the drink made it possible for them to connect on a deeper level. Brad survived not only his own journey with alcoholism, but he'd taken the bottle away from Richard and somehow managed not to drink from it. Of course, maybe there was some magical reasoning to his impulse control.

Natalie nodded. "Good. When are you meeting with him?"

"In an hour."

"Good. Then get your ass to an AA meeting right after."

"I will," he promised.

Remi wished she could go with him, but she had to go to class, and she was already in hot water with her professor. She hoped she could trust him to show up.

"And I'll run an ad for someone to work in the kitchen."

"I don't think that's necessary," Richard said.

"Don't you sass me!" Natalie wagged her finger in his face again.

Remi couldn't help but laugh but choked it back when Natalie's glare landed on her. Her friend could be intimidating when she wanted to be. She turned her attention to her husband.

"Richard, it might not be such a bad idea. Until you get things under control, we could use the extra help."

"Yeah, but I don't know what good that will do when the bottle appears to me in other places. What if it pops up somewhere Emily can reach?"

Natalie shook her head. "That happened when you saw it in the cabinet and ignored it. If you never see it in the first place, nothing should happen. It never did before."

Remi understood where Natalie was coming from, but she wasn't so sure she agreed. The house had shown it could learn before. It was always evolving. At the same time, the alcohol targeted Richard and Richard alone. It shouldn't appear for Emily. When it appeared in her dresser, it was because he was putting her clothes away. If things were anything like before, that shouldn't matter. The house could very well get angry and retaliate. It wouldn't be the first time. It was a risk they needed to take though. Richard needed to keep a clear head, or he could easily succumb to the darkness in the house. He'd been taken over by the alcohol before. Emily had not.

Natalie picked up on her apprehension. "Lucy won't let her drink the liquor even if it does appear."

"Why do you say that?" Richard asked her.

"Well, when I touched Emily this morning to get a feel for everything, it became clear to me that Lucy isn't manipulating her like we originally thought. She does seem to view her as a friend. She's looking out for her."

Remi nodded. She'd been thinking the same recently. Ever since she saw her in the door to the nursery.

"This is Lucy we're talking about," Richard protested.

CHAPTER TWENTY

"She's different now," Remi said. "She's not menacing anymore. She even looks different. Now, it's like she's just a child."

Natalie nodded in agreement. "I can't be sure, but I think it had something to do with the haven stone. It's like it left her here but removed her negative energy. Now, she's the person she was in life."

"I don't understand," Richard shook his head. "How could it remove her negative energy but not all of it? We're all in agreement that what's going on is negative?"

"I don't know," Natalie admitted. "I've been having a hard time getting through to Mel since the first time we talked. There haven't been any updates on that front, but as soon as I reach her, we'll have her on research."

"It's starting to feel like she's ghosted us," Richard grumbled.

Remi and Natalie both stared at him with raised eyebrows.

"No pun intended," he said.

"She hasn't," Natalie insisted. "She's spread thin right now." She paused for a moment before continuing. "I've been considering going out there to see what the hold-up is. Maybe even help her so we can get her here faster."

"What?" Richard asked.

"We need you here!" Remi pleaded.

"Well, that was before last night. I'm too alarmed to go far now."

Remi breathed a sigh of relief. "I hate to cut this short, but I need to get to class, and Richard needs to get to his sponsor."

Natalie nodded. "We can pick this back up later."

Remi kissed Richard. "Really listen to him, okay?"

"I will, babe." He squeezed her hand.

CHAPTER TWENTY-ONE

Remi

Remi barely made it to class on time. She slid into her seat next to Sophia with seconds to spare. The professor glared at her from his place at the front of the room, but he didn't lecture her.

Sophia raised an eyebrow at her, but Remi signaled that she'd tell her about it later. The lecture was beginning.

* * *

When the class was dismissed at the end of the lecture, the professor asked her to stay behind. Remi told Sophia to go ahead without her and waited for the room to empty.

"Mrs. Price, I want to be frank with you," the professor took his seat opposite her at his desk. "At the beginning of the year, I considered you one of my most promising students. You're smart, and you have an excellent grasp of the material.

CHAPTER TWENTY-ONE

Lately, your work has been slipping. You're making mistakes on simple equations, sleeping in class, showing up late or not at all. I have to question your commitment to the program."

"I know I haven't been performing to my full potential," Remi told him. "I really do want this, sir. It's just that there's a lot going on at home. I'll try to do better."

He nodded. "You just had a baby, yes?"

"Yes, sir."

"Perhaps you're spread too thin."

"No, sir. I'm dedicated to everything I do. I didn't quit when I had my first child, and I'm not quitting this time. "

"Well, the thing is, your shoddy work can no longer be ignored, Mrs. Price."

"Am I failing?"

"Not yet. But if you don't score high on your midterm, your grade will suffer."

"I will do well, I promise."

"That will be difficult, Mrs. Price. Midterms have already passed."

Remi sat back as though slapped. It had passed? How had it passed, and she didn't know it? Then she remembered that day when Richard and Natalie found her in the bathroom with Kylie. She didn't go to school that day. Oh God? Was that it?

Remi forced back a sob. "I thought it was next week."

He nodded. "I figured that's what happened. I'm not an unreasonable man, Mrs. Price. I may be persuaded to let you take it tomorrow and say you turned it in on time."

"You'd do that?"

"Of course." He rose to his feet and walked around the desk and leaned back against it. "I'm sympathetic to when my students are having a hard time. I'll help you. But you need to help me."

He unzipped his fly and exposed himself to her.

"Sir?"

He smiled. "Don't be coy. You have two kids. You know what to do." He placed one hand on her head and made to guide her toward him.

Remi slapped his hand away from her. "That's disgusting."

"So is neglecting your work and expecting your professor to turn the other cheek." He grabbed her head and tried to force her toward him again.

Remi slapped his hand again. "If you put that sorry excuse of a prick in my mouth, I will bite it off."

His cheeks blazed with fury. "I would think very hard about this, Mrs. Price. This is your future, after all."

"No, it's yours," a voice said from the doorway. They both looked to see who it was, and Remi smiled triumphantly. Sophia stood in the doorway with her phone raised to the scene.

Remi gathered her things and joined Sophia at the door.

"Give me that," the professor walked toward them. "You don't want to mess with me."

"I think you don't want to mess with me," Sophia smirked, and moved the phone down to get a clear shot of his exposed penis. "I'm the one with the power right now."

The professor glared at her and stuffed himself back in his pants.

"Here's what's going to happen," Sophia said, "you are going to let Remi take a make-up test tomorrow. Unless you want this video sent to the administration, of course. And in case you get any funny ideas in your head, I will be in the room keeping an eye on you."

CHAPTER TWENTY-ONE

"Fine," he spat through gritted teeth.

"Glad to see we're on the same page."

The two girls exited the room, and Remi waited until they were outside the building before hugging her friend. "Thank you so much. How'd you know?"

"I had a bad feeling. I've never liked the way he looks at you."

"I love that you showed up, but I really wish you hadn't blackmailed him. It kind of negates the win."

"Psst." Sophia laughed. "It's not blackmail. I'm sending the video to the administration regardless. He's a vile pig. I'm going to wait until after your test."

Remi smiled. "I don't know what I'd do without you."

Sophia winked. "You're never going to have to find out, chick."

CHAPTER TWENTY-TWO

Remi

Remi's good mood shattered when she walked in the front door and saw Natalie standing in the parlor. She was bursting with fury as she looked into the face of the suited man opposite her.

"What's going on?" Remi asked.

"Remi Huang?" The man asked without waiting for an introduction.

"It's Remi Price now," she corrected.

"Please, have a seat." He gestured toward the sofa and took a seat in a cushy armchair opposite.

Was this stranger inviting her to sit in her own home?

"Maybe you should tell me who you are and what this is about. Then I'll consider sitting down."

"Alright," the man's lips were set in a tight line. "I'm Dominic Flannagan. Child Protective Services."

What? Remi grabbed the back of a chair for support and took a quick look around. There weren't too many guests roaming around, thankfully. She stepped forward and took a seat on the sofa. Natalie sat next to her and took her hand.

CHAPTER TWENTY-TWO

Her friend had a vise grip as if trying to convey some sort of message.

Mr. Flannagan looked down at his clipboard. "We got an anonymous report of severe child abuse in this residence."

What? Remi thought again. Her girls were so spoiled. This did not make sense.

"That's ridiculous," Natalie said for her. "This house is always full of people, and anyone could tell you how adored those kids are."

"What kind of allegations have been made?" Remi asked.

"The person we spoke with posed several situations. They said that you are either on drugs or need mental help. They allege that they overheard you say you wanted to bash your daughter's head in with a fireplace poker."

Remi went to shoot to her feet, but Natalie grabbed her and pulled her back down. The lies! When she found out who said such a horrible thing, they'd be in for a world of hurt.

"They also allege that you tried to hold your baby underwater."

"I can vouch for her there," Natalie cut in. "Remi has a sleepwalking condition she wasn't aware of. She was in the bathroom with the baby, but the baby was NOT in the tub. Remi is now seeing a doctor for the condition and preventative measures are being taken to ensure it doesn't happen again."

Remi wished Natalie hadn't said this. She'd told Doctor Taylor a different story, and she didn't know if the discrepancy would bite her in the ass.

Mr. Flannagan nodded. "We'll need to contact the physician's office to verify. They also made comments that your husband has an alcohol problem."

"My husband has struggled with alcohol in the past, but he

is in AA and is actually with his sponsor right now. He was also never violent while drinking."

"They also expressed concern about the children being in a house with strangers who have access to their bedrooms."

"We do run a bed & breakfast, as you can see," Remi said. "However, we have separate family quarters and it's behind a locked door. No one can access the children without us knowing."

"Alright. Would you mind giving me a tour of the house, including the children's bedrooms?"

"Does she have to?" Natalie asked.

"No. I can come back with an order, but it'll look better for you if you comply now."

Natalie was about to protest again, but Remi cut her off. "It's alright, Nat. I don't have anything to hide."

Remi led the investigator from room to room on the first floor before leading him upstairs. She didn't take him into any of the guest rooms since they were all occupied, but she led him into the family wing.

He spent extra time studying Emily's bedroom and the nursery. He talked to Emily for a few minutes and asked her about her drawings before they all went back downstairs.

Once they were back on the front porch, Mr. Flannagan turned back to Remi. "Well, from what I can see, this appears to be a malicious complaint. The children are well fed, clean, and provided with all their necessities and more. I'm going to make a note in your file and close the case for now. I must warn you, they were quite insistent there was an issue, so another claim may be filed."

"So, who was it?" Remi asked.

"I can't tell you that," he told her. "It was anonymous. I'm merely telling you that when someone goes out of their way to list off this many unsubstantiated claims, it's rare for them to let it go."

They thanked the man and let him go on his way.

"It was clearly my parents," Remi said when he was out of hearing range. "My dad accused me of being on drugs the night he was kicked out."

"I don't know," Natalie shook her head. "I didn't get anything clear when I shook his hand. But your parents did know about Margaret. The house's history is common knowledge, but Margaret and Gloria are not. Also, they never knew about Richard's drinking problem."

"Well, who was it then?"

Natalie shook her head. "I don't know but something about this whole situation is fishy. I don't like it when I can't pick anything up. It isn't normal."

CHAPTER TWENTY-THREE

Margaret

Margaret sat on the floor in the parlor covered in gore. She put her back to the wall and rocked repeatedly. Her eyes were glassed over as they fixed on a spot on the wall.

She heard a door open in the distance but didn't move to see who entered.

"Oh my God," a voice said from the foyer. Soft footsteps walked into the parlor and a person knelt in front of her.

It was Beau Thompson, who lived at the neighboring plantation, Heaven's Estate. "Margaret?" He waved a hand in front of her eyes to check for any reaction. "Margaret? Are you hurt?"

"She—she did it," Percy squeaked. He stood behind Beau, who turned to look at him. He didn't react negatively. He didn't react at all.

Beau turned back to Margaret and clapped his hands in front of her face. She flinched, and the fog lifted. She blinked her eyes several times and looked around the room.

"Margaret? Margaret, look at me," Beau commanded with

CHAPTER TWENTY-THREE

gentle authority.

She looked into his eyes and calm spread through her body. It was going to be okay. Somehow, she knew that with her whole soul.

"Beau?"

"Did you have an intruder?"

"I—I don't know," Margaret's voice shook slightly. It wasn't a lie. Her mind was a fog. She'd seen a horrific scene unfold in front of her eyes. One where she'd been the perpetrator, but it hadn't felt real. Her feelings for needing to get rid of the youngest were real. But she'd never hurt Josie or Lucy. Never. Still, her son was standing as far away from her as he could, behind Beau, sobbing.

She looked down at her body and breathed in deeply. Her arms were solid red with blood, she could feel it everywhere else now, and she couldn't see what color her dress was. A fireplace poker lay across her lap with a suspicious clump of blood, hair, and something else. Her stomach emptied onto the floor next to her.

Beau gently took the poker from her lap and slid it behind him out of her reach.

"I don't know!" she insisted, and tears streamed down her face.

"Okay. Okay." Beau got to his feet and held out his hands to help her to hers. "Come here."

He led her into the hallway, and she recoiled at the sight she saw. Josie and both the girls lay dead on the floor. It hadn't been a dream. Oh God. What had she done?

She screamed and turned to run, but Beau grabbed her arm and jerked back.

Margaret turned her head into Beau's shoulder. He gently

pulled her head up to look him in the eye. "Margaret, did you do this?"

"I didn't mean to," she cried. "I swear I didn't."

Beau looked back to the bodies. "Who is the other girl?"

Margaret couldn't bring herself to tell him. She'd made it so long without admitting where the girl came from.

"She's our sister," Percy told him.

Margaret wanted to snap at him. He knew that fact wasn't supposed to leave the walls of the house, but she didn't have the energy to scold him. She merely closed her eyes. The cat was out of the bag now. She let out a sorrowful wail.

Beau raised an eyebrow. She'd have to tell him something now. It might as well be the truth.

"The soldiers," she said with shame.

He inclined his head, and his eyes were soft. Thank goodness he wasn't going to make her go into detail. He knew what she meant. He'd known the soldiers were at Blackwood Manor. Thankfully, there was no judgement on his face. It could have been so much worse.

"Help me. Brother," she whispered. "Please help me."

"Okay, well, the first order of business is the bodies."

"John's coming home. He can't know. Oh, God." She jerked her head to the door as if expecting him to walk in on the horrific scene at that very moment.

"It doesn't have to go beyond this room."

She furrowed her brow in confusion.

"Scarlet fever is going around. We can say they passed from that. No one will question it. We have to bury them."

Margaret knelt by Lucy's cold body and pulled it into her lap. "No one knows about the other one," she told Beau. "Three graves will raise questions. Plus," she pulled Lucy to her chest

CHAPTER TWENTY-THREE

in a gruesome embrace, "I need to keep her close to me. Please."

Beau bit his lip and surveyed the space around them. "I have an idea. It's a bit out there."

"What is it?"

"We can put the other girl in Lucy's grave. But we'd have to entomb Lucy in the house."

Margaret nodded. "Do it."

Percy stood in the doorway of the parlor watching the scene with a ghostly white face.

Beau took Lucy from Margaret's arms and carried her into the parlor where he laid her gently on the floor. He walked back to them. "I'm going to go out to the cemetery and start digging graves." He turned his attention to Percy. "You're a big boy, and she's small. Do you think you can carry her for me?"

Percy nodded and walked forward cautiously. He pulled the girl into his arms and whispered, "I'm so sorry," in her hair. Beau cradled Josie into his arms and looked at Margaret. "Start cleaning up the blood." Then Beau and Percy walked to the rear exit to carry the bodies out.

Margaret looked down at the bloody mess around her and sighed as she removed her dress. She knew she should feel shame to stand in the foyer in her underthings when a man who wasn't her husband was on the property, but he was occupied outside, and all she could think of was getting clean.

She did her best to avoid the blood on the floor as she made her way to the cellar. Josie kept a washbasin down there to clean the girl with, and it was the nearest one.

Margaret washed the blood from her skin as best she could and retrieved fresh water and cleaning supplies to go to work cleaning the floor and walls upstairs.

When she was finished, she washed the blood from her hair and put on a fresh dress. All that remained on the lower level was her bloody dress and Lucy's body lying in the parlor.

It didn't feel real, and she thanked her lucky stars that her brother was here for her now. She'd barely spoken to her family since marrying John, and she hadn't even known that Beau wasn't at war. What a blessing that he came so swiftly, and that he didn't ask questions. There was no judgement. If her father were here, he'd still be talking about what a disgrace she was.

Now, as she waited on Beau and Percy to return, she wondered if this would remain a secret.

CHAPTER TWENTY-FOUR

Margaret

Margaret lost track of how many days she was locked in her bedroom. Coping with everything that happened proved too difficult.

Despite his acting out and obvious hatred for her, Percy was amazing about the whole thing. He didn't push himself into her personal space. He didn't knock on her door demanding hugs and stories. He did leave food outside her door every day, but she barely touched it.

It was hard to have an appetite when she thought about everything she'd done. She'd spent her entire life trying to be a good person, and up until now, she'd thought she was. A good person wouldn't do what she'd done.

She'd taken three lives. Three. What kind of person did something like that? Thoughts of the demon nestled inside the young girl no longer crossed her mind. It was as if those thoughts were never there. Instead, she thought of how small the girl was, her sunken in cheeks, her large eyes, the rags she wore. She thought about her sleeping on the hard ground in the cellar and how little she'd allowed her to eat. She was a monster.

Clarity was something Margaret got plenty of while she was locked away in her room. She was the demon. She'd let darkness into her heart and let it play with her mind. It was her all along. The girl was a girl. All she'd done was be born, and what Margaret did to her was nothing short of torture.

All that was bad enough, but her actions on that night showed how weak she really was. She'd let it in. She'd been so thoroughly tricked. John wasn't coming home. Not now, anyway. When everything was over, and she'd gone back to her room, the letter she'd received was now blank. It was an illusion.

And Lucy? It shouldn't have surprised her that Lucy had been to the cellar. She'd always loved the younger girl, playing dollies, building forts, and playing tag. She embraced her role as a big sister. Of course, it wouldn't stop simply because Margaret banished the girl to the cellar.

Margaret could have sworn it was the younger girl! But she realized now that was a trick too. The girls looked alike, but the younger one was smaller. Much, much smaller. It should have been apparent that she was not the one to emerge from the cellar that night.

Then there was Josie. Her best friend, her confidant, and, however briefly, her lover. She'd been a beautiful spirit, and she made Margaret want to be a better person. She'd put everything on the line and tried to protect the little girl to the best of her ability, even if it meant destroying their relationship. It wasn't her fault she'd been unsuccessful.

Margaret rolled onto her side and wept uncontrollably. How? How could she have done this? She'd lost everything. Percy knew what she'd done, and he hated her. He might not

CHAPTER TWENTY-FOUR

willfully disobey her anymore, out of fear, and he may have quietly told her once that it wasn't her fault, but he hated her. She could see it on his face. It was only a matter of time before the war was over, and John came home for real. Percy would tell him. Her days were numbered.

Margaret thought back to that day that seemed so long ago now. The one where Percy asked her, "What if we're next?" She'd believed him to be a disrespectful snot at that moment, but he'd been right. He could still be right.

Something in this house made her do what she'd done. It latched on to her biggest fears and showed them to her over and over again until she'd believed they were real. Yes, things settled down since, but she still felt that ominous presence. It filled the air of the room and breathed against her cheek when she was on the verge of sleep.

In a particularly weak moment, Margaret wrote a confession letter to John. She planned to hang herself in the attic.

But then she remembered it was only her and Percy left in the house. Who would care for him if she did something like that? She also didn't want him to walk in on the scene. The poor boy had seen enough death. He didn't need more. So, she abandoned the idea and hid the letter in the back of Lucy's portrait.

Fear loomed in Margaret's mind every waking moment. She was terrified that she'd hurt someone again. Finally, she decided she needed to bear her cross silently. But she made a vow to never let herself get close to anyone again.

CHAPTER TWENTY-FIVE

Remi

"The nerve!" Richard growled that night at dinner.

Remi told him about the CPS visit as soon as he got home, and he'd been in a bad mood ever since. She'd briefly considered not telling him. Mr. Flannagan said he was closing the case, after all. Natalie convinced her it was better to say something now, in case it did persist in the future.

Gus sat uncomfortably. Remi gave him an apologetic smile before returning to her food. Gus didn't do well with confrontation. Ever since the paranormal group found out he was a member of the Wilkes family from Heaven's Estate in disguise, and he'd been put on the spot, he'd excused himself from any situation that could be considered tense.

After everything was all said and done, Gus hadn't been able to bring himself to go back to Heaven's Estate, even though he was now the rightful owner. He said he couldn't live somewhere that was behind so many dark acts. He'd even elected to keep his assumed name.

Richard turned to Natalie. "Have we heard anything from Mel? Can you get her to figure out where Malaki and Mira

CHAPTER TWENTY-FIVE

are? I think I need to have a talk with the man."

Remi grabbed her husband's arm and squeezed it. "Let it go."

"What? Babe, no," he turned to her. "Do you not understand what happened here? He tried to have our kids taken away."

"Natalie said she didn't think it was him."

They'd already been over this a couple of times. Remi could admit it was her initial thought too, but some of the complaints were based on things her parents simply didn't know.

"Oh, come on. 'You're either on drugs or mentally unstable?' He accused you of both!"

"There's something more going on," Natalie said simply.

Richard turned to her with flashing eyes. "I want to talk to Mel, regardless. I'm starting to think you haven't reached out to her at all."

"Richard!" Remi admonished. "What is wrong with you?"

"Why the hell would I keep you from talking to Mel?" Natalie asked, never the one to back down from a challenge. "What do I have to gain from it?"

He rose to his feet, and his voice boomed across the kitchen in a way that made Remi's skin crawl. "I don't know, but it's suspicious as hell. You're the only one that talked to her, and she's suspiciously said she'll show up, but it hasn't happened yet?"

Natalie's hand shot across the table, and she grabbed his wrist before he could pull it back. Her eyes narrowed coolly, and she released him. "Damn it. You just came from your sponsor. Have you no self-control?"

Remi looked at him with hurt eyes. "You drank again already?"

He set his lips in a fine line. "Well, what do you expect?

You women are driving me nuts because you don't have any common sense!"

Remi instinctively grabbed his arm, and he swung out with the other. His hand hit her cheek hard when he made contact. Surprised, she lost her balance and tumbled to the floor. Her chin bounced off the tile, causing her to bite her tongue.

Her mouth filled with blood as she caught a flash of white light in her peripheral vision. Richard landed with a thump on his butt on the floor.

"Stop it! Stop it!" Emily cried.

Remi felt hands on her shoulders helping her to her feet. "Remi, are you okay?"

"Yeah," Remi spat blood on the floor to clear her airway.

Natalie glared at Richard across the room. "You keep your ass in the cottage until this gets sorted out."

"You can't kick me out of my own house," he snarled.

"Watch me," she snarled right back.

He rolled his eyes, muttered, "This isn't over," and stormed out the back door.

Remi rushed to Emily and moved to pull her out of her highchair, but the girl stuck her hands out and squealed, "Stay away! Stay away!"

"You're a bloody mess," Natalie whispered and put a reassuring hand on her shoulder. "Why don't you go get cleaned up, and I'll calm her down? Meet us in her room in twenty minutes?"

Remi glanced around the room and noted the shocked expressions Gus and Jessie wore. How embarrassing.

Twenty minutes later, scrubbed clean from a shower, and wearing a fresh blouse, Remi entered her daughter's bedroom.

Emily lay in the crook of Natalie's arm, staring down at a

picture book. Her eyes were still puffy from crying, but she wasn't wailing anymore, which was a significant improvement.

"Knock, knock," Remi said gently. "Can I come in?"

Emily nodded, but she held onto Natalie tighter.

Remi grabbed a chair and set it at the foot of the bed so she could get down to her daughter's level without getting too close. "Can we talk about what happened?"

Emily looked up. "You and Daddy were mean. He hurt you."

Remi sighed. "Yes. I'm sorry about that. We never should have been mean to each other, especially in front of you. And Daddy didn't mean to hurt me. He was scared."

Remi cringed at the words coming out of her mouth. She'd hoped she wouldn't need to have such a serious conversation with Emily at this age, but this had happened, and it needed to be addressed.

"Why was he scared?"

"Do you remember that man who came to visit today?"

Emily nodded.

"Well, he came because someone said we aren't a good mommy and daddy to you and baby Kylie. He had to make sure you were okay. Daddy was upset that someone said something so mean."

"He was sad?"

"Yes. He was sad."

Emily thought for a minute. "Lucy say you hurt me."

Remi sighed again. When Emily told her that the first time, she'd assumed it was a threat. Now, she needed to consider it could be a warning.

"Did Lucy say how?"

"The man," Lucy said from over her shoulder.

Remi and Natalie both jumped and spun toward the voice.

Lucy sat on the floor in front of the closet door with her legs folded under her.

Remi forced down her fear and spoke to the girl.

"What do you mean?"

"That man who was here," Lucy clarified. "He's a bad person. He stirred up the negative energy, and they fed on it. Now, they're stronger and turning you against each other."

"I don't understand."

Lucy got to her feet and walked to Remi so that they were eye to eye.

"It's what they do. I was a victim of it once. They took my mixed-up feelings about my mother and made me hateful."

"So," Remi said cautiously, "you're saying something here is using the strained relationship between me and my dad to—"

"To make you angry. To make your husband angry. Because then, you're not as much of a threat. You'll eventually forget the way you are, and anything other than what they want you to believe."

"So, what do we do?" Natalie asked.

Lucy turned her gaze to her. "You were on the right track before. You need that stone that you used before."

"But it didn't work," Remi furrowed her eyebrows.

"It weakened them. You need more strength and to go a little longer."

Remi flew to her feet, ran to her bedroom, and threw open the closet door. Natalie followed her and asked her what she was doing as she pulled a shoebox off the top shelf.

"We packed away the haven stone for safekeeping, in case we ever needed it again." Remi opened the shoebox, and her eyes went wide when she saw the stone was not there. "No. No, no, no. It was in here!" Remi pointed a finger at the box, willing the stone to appear.

"Could it be in another box?" Natalie asked.

"I don't think so," Remi said, but she turned back to the closet to grab another box.

When that box didn't turn up anything either, Remi shredded the tissue that was inside and moved to start pulling out more stuff.

"Hold on, hold on," Natalie chuckled and stepped forward. "Before you turn the whole house into a cyclone."

Natalie put her hands to the surface of every item in the closet, making sure to take extra care as she went. Emily walked into the room and curled up on the bed to watch.

"You using your magic power, Aunt Natawie?"

"Uh huh," Natalie answered, and kept moving until she was satisfied the stone was not in the closet. She went to the bed and picked up the original box Remi said the stone was in.

Finally, she set it down and looked at Remi. "You might want to sit down for this."

"Oh God," Remi thought. She couldn't take anything else going wrong right now. But she still did as her friend said and took a seat on the bed.

"Do you want the good news or the bad news first?"

"Let's start with the good."

"Okay. The good news is you were right. It was in the closet, and it was in this box. Congratulations. You're not crazy."

"So, what's the bad news?"

Natalie sighed. "Jamie has it."

Jamie? Remi sat back and ran a hand through her hair. She hadn't been expecting that, but it did make sense. Jamie was enamored with the stone back in the day. She'd been the one to find it and was completely captivated.

"She took it the night she left," Natalie answered, seeing the question in her eyes.

"She came in while we were *sleeping*?" Now that was a little creepy. Jamie left in the middle of the night. They'd seen her at dinner. The next morning, she was gone. Richard drove around for a while looking for her, and Mel checked for rental cars or motels, but she hadn't been in either one of those.

"I guess she really wanted out of here," Natalie said quietly.

That kind of hurt. Remi considered them friends. She knew Jamie thought she was a little privileged, and compared to her background, she was. But the girl still confided in Remi about the abuse and neglect she'd endured at the hands of her father and stepmother.

Remi knew what Natalie was referring to. Jamie was claustrophobic. She even slept with a night light. So, for her to come into their bedroom at night, in the dark, and rummage around in the closet was highly unusual. Rod's death affected them all, but no one as much as Jamie.

* * *

Ten minutes later, Remi sat on the bed with Emily cradled in her lap. The young girl was fighting sleep, but she hadn't started throwing a tantrum yet.

"Scared, Mommy," Emily whispered and buried her face into Remi's breast.

"I know, baby." Remi sighed and kissed the top of her daughter's head. She didn't know what she was supposed

CHAPTER TWENTY-FIVE

to do. They both needed sleep but something in the house was trying to drive them all apart, and it used their dream state to do it.

As if in answer to her prayers, a small voice spoke from beside her. "I'll stay with her if you want. I won't let anything happen to her."

Remi turned to face Lucy who sat cross-legged on her other side. The girl looked at her with soft eyes.

"I thought you were the one being mean to her."

Lucy shook her head. "I can see why you'd think that. I sit in front of her closet to try and stand guard. It's the other one. She did it to me too. She's a vicious person and seems nice at first. Until she starts telling you to do awful things."

"That's what she's doing to Emily?"

Lucy nodded. "I gave in. I wish I hadn't. Maybe things would have been different. Emily's got a stronger mind, though. She knows what she's being told is wrong, and she's resisting. Eventually, she'll crumble. She's tired."

Remi looked down at Emily's little face. Her eyes fluttered closed, then she jerked them open again. She was two years old and trying to fight sleep because she was too afraid of what could happen when she slept. Something needed to change.

"Can you stop the other one?"

"No," Lucy admitted. "She has too much power. But I can alert you immediately."

That would have to be good enough for Remi. She gathered Emily in her arms, walked to her bedroom, and gently laid her in the bed.

"No," Emily half whispered without opening her eyes.

"It's okay, baby. Lucy's going to stay with you tonight, and you're going to have a slumber party."

Emily didn't answer her. She was finally out.

Remi turned to Lucy and thanked her before going back to her own room.

She entered as Natalie was hanging up the phone.

"Did you finally reach her?" Remi asked as she collapsed on the bed.

"Yeah," Natalie ran a hand through her hair. "Only took about ten calls. She's going to come, but she can't stay long."

"How come?"

"Something's going on at Hotel Dahlia. It used to be passive but now something is frightening the guests."

Remi nodded. She knew that wasn't normal for the hotel. Mel told her before that she'd loved growing up there and despite the activity, it always felt like a peaceful place. She'd even said it was a blessing to have so many guardian angels.

"Did Emily actually go down without argument?"

"Lucy's keeping watch."

Natalie raised an eyebrow and gave her a crooked grin. "You have a ghost babysitting?"

"Emily's comfortable with her. And she'll let us know if something happens. Now that she knows we don't hate her anymore."

"I guess that's true," Natalie said. "I called Dani too. I told her I was going to stay here tonight."

Dani was Natalie's girlfriend. They'd started off as roommates but eventually progressed to more. Dani was the one who referred Richard to Natalie.

"You don't have to do that. I'm about to knock out. I'm exhausted."

"I know I don't have to. I'd feel more comfortable. Just in case Richard decides to come back in."

CHAPTER TWENTY-FIVE

Remi didn't think he would. If she knew her husband, he would be sitting out there beating himself up over what happened. He'd had time to cool down. Still, things have been unpredictable lately, and it couldn't hurt to have back up.

"Thanks."

Natalie nodded and grabbed one of Remi's nightgowns from the dresser to change for the night.

CHAPTER TWENTY-SIX

Margaret

When the War ended, Margaret was a bundle of nerves. She'd been a shut-in for so long, and she knew her way of life was about to change.

Looking out the window and seeing soldiers walking down the lane as they made their way home filled her with dread.

The woman she used to be would have rolled up her sleeves and offered them a place to sleep for the night and a hot meal, but that was an inconceivable thought now. She would never be able to bring soldiers into her home after what happened to her and Josie. It didn't matter that they were Confederate. She didn't want them here.

When she saw one of them coming, Margaret would dart behind the nearest door and hide. Sometimes a knock on the door would come. Sometimes it wouldn't.

Once, she'd been surprised to walk downstairs and find the front door wide open. Percy sat on the front steps next to a man in a tattered uniform with a knapsack. The man was eating a sandwich and drinking a glass of milk while Percy prattled on about books.

CHAPTER TWENTY-SIX

"Percy!" she'd admonished. "Come here this instant!"

The boy jumped to his feet with wide eyes and came to her side. She grabbed his arm and pulled him into the house.

"I'm sorry to scare you, ma'am," the soldier said. "I don't mean no harm. Your boy was kind enough to offer me something to eat. You've raised him right."

"You may finish your meal," Margaret told him, "but you can't stay here. It isn't proper."

"Yes, ma'am. Of course, ma'am."

Margaret slammed the door without another word and turned to her son. "Just what do you think you're doing? We don't know this man."

"He's returning from the War," Percy protested. "He was almost crawling down the road, and he looked so pitiful and hungry. I didn't think it would hurt to help him get his energy back up."

Margaret sighed and put a hand on Percy's shoulder. "Son, I love your heart. But things aren't the way they were before. You can't do that again."

He'd nodded, hung his head and trudged up the stairs. Margaret's heart broke with the realization that their relationship was deteriorating day by day.

She had a true test of spirit the day she'd heard the front door slam open when she'd been in the kitchen. She'd stopped what she was doing, barely daring to breathe. That sound would always remind her of two horrible nights. The night the soldiers first came, and the night she'd lost her family.

"Margaret? Children?"

John. It was John's voice carrying through the empty house. Her husband was home. Margaret dried her hands and ran out to the foyer.

He stood looking into the parlor. There were massive holes in his uniform, and he was much too skinny, but he was home.

"John?"

He turned to her. His eyes brightened, and he smiled wide behind his scraggly beard. "I'm home, my love."

Margaret launched herself into his arms. She'd doubted she'd ever see him again, that he'd ever come home. But here he was, holding her tight to him, and she could feel his steady heartbeat against hers.

He pulled back and gave her a long kiss. Oh, it was glorious. He was home. Her John. All was right with the world. But then, she remembered. He was going to look at her differently when he learned what happened. He wasn't going to want her anymore. Because she didn't deserve to be happy.

Her smile fell, and he frowned at her. "What's wrong, my love?"

She shook her head and tried to force a smile for his sake. "It doesn't feel real. I expect I'll open my eyes and find it was all a dream."

He smiled again. "I assure you. I'm very real." He kissed her again, long and hard. "Where are the children?"

She'd hoped that question wouldn't come so quickly, and they'd have time to enjoy each other before the harsh reality hit.

Margaret swallowed and looked up into his eyes. "Percy is at Heaven's Estate playing. And Lucy—" Tears welled in her eyes as she let out a choked sob.

John stepped back and the brightness was gone from his eyes. "What? What about Lucy?"

"She's gone." She forced herself to say it. She couldn't beat around the bush. She couldn't pretend that their daughter

CHAPTER TWENTY-SIX

was still alive, and they were going to be a family, happily ever after.

"How?"

She nearly told him the truth. She knew Percy would do so when he came home. It would be better coming from her. But she couldn't bear to look him in the eye and see his expression turn to hate.

Beau Thompson's lie popped into her head and slid off her tongue before she could stop it. "Scarlet fever. Her and Josie both. The servants left long ago. It's only me and Percy now."

John's back hit the wall, and he let out a sorrowful wail. "Our girl!" Then he held out his arms, pulled her into an embrace, and they cried together.

CHAPTER TWENTY-SEVEN

Remi

An eerie tune woke Remi up. She didn't open her eyes immediately. The longer she laid there with her eyes squeezed tightly shut, the more her heart raced. The music was coming from close by and had an extremely old timey sound.

Remi forced herself to open her eyes and roll over to face where the music was coming from, ignoring the bells tinkling on her wrists.

An old-fashioned music box sat on the dresser. The lid was up and the ballerina inside was dancing to the depressing rhythm. Remi shot up and stared at it. She'd seen this music box before. It appeared in the parlor when the group first returned to the house after a police investigation. No one had ever seen it before or knew where it came from.

It hadn't played back then, though. It only sat on the credenza mocking them. It disappeared after that day, and they hadn't given it another thought.

Remi turned on her lamp and got out of bed to examine it. She was about to reach for it when a hand grasped her arm.

CHAPTER TWENTY-SEVEN

She jumped and turned to Natalie. She'd forgotten her friend was there. Natalie shook her head and took a cautious step toward the box.

Remi's heart beat faster when she saw the key in the front. This was the kind of music box that needed to be wound to play.

Natalie placed a hand to the side of the box. The music stopped, then the key began to turn.

Remi bolted for the door and flung it open. As soon as she reached the hallway, a scream tore through the night.

"Remi! Remi!" Natalie ran after her. "Are you alright?"

"It wasn't me."

Another scream echoed down the hallway, and they raced toward it.

CHAPTER TWENTY-EIGHT

Margaret

"Percy, what's wrong, son?" John's voice carried out Percy's bedroom door, and Margaret stood in the hall holding her breath and straining her ears to listen.

"You haven't been the same since I came home."

He hadn't been. Percy had always been a quiet child, but more so now than ever. Margaret expected him to tell John immediately, but three months had passed now, and he still hadn't uttered a word about it.

"It's just—" Percy said. "Everything's different now. The house is different, you're different. Mama's different."

"War does change things," John agreed. "When you add losing your sister and Josie into the situation, you have to understand your mother is going to be grieving for a long time."

Margaret's heart thundered. Was this it? Was this where she was going to be tossed out of the house? Or would he do to her what she'd done to Lucy?

"It's not just that. Soldiers came. In the night. And took over the house. They stole, they broke things. They were really

CHAPTER TWENTY-EIGHT

mean to Mama and Josie."

"*Oh God! Oh God!*" Margaret's head swam.

"That must have been scary," John said.

"It was. Mama hasn't been the same since. She doesn't spend time with me. She doesn't hug or kiss. Sometimes, I think she hates me."

"*Oh no, sweet boy,*" Margaret thought. "*I can't let myself get close again. That dark thing might try to take over again.*"

"Well, at least it's not just me," John chuckled. "She'll be okay. You need to give her time. The more things get back to normal, you'll see her return."

The bed creaked as he stood up. "Oh, I've been meaning to ask you, son. What happened to your floor over there? That big stain? Did you hurt yourself?"

Margaret closed her eyes and thought back to that night. She'd scrubbed the hell out of the foyer when cleaning up the blood, and not a trace of it remained. She couldn't remember if she'd cleaned upstairs. Had Percy cleaned his floor himself? Oh, her poor boy.

There was a pause, and then, "I tripped over a toy and got a nosebleed."

"That's a big nosebleed."

"It broke my nose."

"Are you okay now?

"Yes. It was a long time ago."

"Alright. Well, the blood probably won't come up after so long. I'll see what I can do about fixing the floor tomorrow, alright?"

CHAPTER TWENTY-NINE

Remi

"I don't care if it is your property!" the male guest, Mr. Henderson thundered. "It is absolutely unacceptable to let yourselves into a guest's room to play up the ghost nonsense this place is known for!" He sat down on the bed and pulled his wife to him. The poor woman was still shaking like a leaf.

"I'm so sorry," Remi apologized again and looked around the room.

"Sorry isn't good enough!" the man snarled. "While we were sleeping? While we were *sleeping*?"

Remi took in the dark streaks of the symbols that were sloppily drawn on the walls and ceiling in a red substance that looked horribly like blood. "Mr. Henderson. I don't know who did this, but I can assure you it was not anyone on our staff."

"I don't give a good God damn who it was!" the man roared.

"Folks, everything is fine. Please, go back to your rooms," Gus's voice trailed in from the hallway. Remi asked him to stand outside and keep anyone calm who might come to

CHAPTER TWENTY-NINE

investigate.

"You need to calm down," Natalie said cooly from where she stood in the corner with her arms crossing her chest.

"Calm down? Calm down? Don't tell me to calm down, missy," he shook his finger at Natalie. "This is completely unacceptable."

"Screaming about it doesn't do anyone any good," Natalie countered.

"I'll be happy to move you to another room," Remi tried to pacify him.

"No way in hell. We want our money back. Not only for tonight, but for the duration of our trip! And you will pay for a cab to take us into the city and find other accommodations!"

"Fine," Remi agreed. "Gus!"

Gus stepped in from the hallway and threw one last look over his shoulder.

"Take Mr. Henderson downstairs and refund his stay. I'm going to help Mrs. Henderson pack their things."

"But we're no refunds," Gus protested.

Mr. Henderson growled and took a step toward Gus.

"It's the computer system," Gus said evenly. "The programming only does refunds in the event of a cancellation."

"Give it to him from the till," Remi told him. "I'll figure it out later. Put an extra twenty on top of it for a cab."

The two men exited the room, and Remi turned back to Mrs. Henderson, ignoring the pointed look Natalie shot her. The woman looked so tiny sitting perched on the end of the bed. She wore a yellow nightgown, and her arms wrapped around herself.

Remi got to her knees so she could look into the woman's eyes. "Did you see anything Mrs. Henderson?"

She hadn't been able to ask questions while Mr. Henderson was in the room, due to the man's yelling and demands. She couldn't blame him though. If she'd woken up to that sight, she would have felt violated too.

"There was a shadow," the woman whispered. "A big one. It filled the whole doorway of the closet." She pointed to the closet for emphasis.

Remi walked over and looked inside. The door was open, but there was nothing there. The couple didn't even have any clothes on the hangers.

Natalie followed her to the closet and placed her hands to the woodwork on either side of the door frame.

"It was gone when I turned on the light," Mrs. Henderson went on, "then I saw—" her voice cracked, and she closed her eyes.

"I'm so sorry that happened. I wish there was something I could say that could change it." Remi went to the woman and put a reassuring hand on her shoulder. "We'll step outside so you can change, then I'll help you gather your things."

"No!" the woman grabbed Remi's arm when she turned for the door. "Please don't leave me. I don't want to be in this room alone!"

Remi understood the fear. This was her bedroom before she got together with Richard and they'd created the family wing. She'd had a terrifying experience of her own in this room the very first night she slept in it. Instead of arguing, Remi nodded and walked to the corner with Natalie to face the wall while Mrs. Henderson changed.

* * *

CHAPTER TWENTY-NINE

An hour later, Remi, Natalie, and Gus returned to the room. They'd listened to Mr. Henderson ranting for a while longer while they waited for a cab, which took longer than normal due to the late hour.

Gus put his hands on his hips and sighed. "Well, I guess I better get to work and clean this up."

"No, leave it for a while," Natalie told him. "I want to examine every square inch of this room."

"It could stain," he protested. "We don't know what was used to make the markings.

"I'll clean it up," Natalie told him. "If it stains, I'll paint over it myself."

Gus excused himself from the room and closed the door behind him.

"Did you pick up anything from the door?" Remi asked.

Natalie nodded. "And from the music box. It was the same entity. A very large, dark mass."

"It must be the same man Nadine was talking about."

"Actually, it was more feminine energy."

Remi furrowed her eyebrows. "But not an actual form?"

"No," Natalie sighed. "And that's why I want to go over every inch of this room. So, this is going to be a long and tedious process but stick with me. After I finish a section and move on to the next, photograph the symbols for Mel. Make sure you get all the symbols. We don't know what could end up being important."

"You got it." Remi reached into her robe pocket and pulled out her cell phone.

CHAPTER THIRTY

Remi

Remi never got a chance to go back to bed that night. They were about a quarter of the way through their meticulous work investigating the room when the baby monitor crackled. Kylie was awake, and it wasn't too long before Emily followed suit. Remi called down for Gus, who promptly ran up the stairs and took her place taking photographs so she could tend to the girls.

Now, Remi sat at the kitchen table fighting sleep with a steaming cup of coffee in front of her. Emily was perched in her highchair, babbling happily as she stuffed pieces of a pancake in her mouth.

There was a tentative knock on the back door and Richard stuck his head inside. "Can I come in?" Remi took a good, long look at her husband. He certainly looked like himself now. There was none of that dark hatred that was in his eyes last night.

"Are you going to be a dick?" Natalie shot back at him from her spot at the table. She'd finished upstairs a few minutes before and helped herself to a serving of pancakes and eggs.

CHAPTER THIRTY

Remi flicked her eyes to Emily. Her adorable daughter normally let them know if they used inappropriate language in front of her, but she appeared blissfully unaware at the moment. She must not know the word "dick" yet. Thank God for small favors.

Richard shook his head and walked inside. He took a seat at the table next to Remi. "Look at me, please."

She faced him, and his hand tenderly brushed her cheek. "Does it hurt?"

Remi shook her head. It hurt like hell all night, but not anymore. Maybe it was the chaos of the Henderson's late-night visitor, but she hadn't felt it in hours. Somehow, she hadn't even bruised.

"I'm so sorry, Remi," Richard told her and lifted her hand to kiss it. "I don't know what happened. That wasn't me. You have to know that."

"It's the alcohol," Natalie snapped. "That's why we've gone out of our way to help you and try to keep you from going down that road. God, I fucking hate drunks."

"Aunt Natawie!"

Natalie smiled at the girl, but that smile didn't quite reach her eyes. Remi knew that drinking was a sensitive topic for Natalie. Her own father was a drunk and disappeared from her life when she was only nine years old. He'd resurfaced years later claiming he'd never done such a thing.

Richard nodded. "I called my sponsor last night. We talked for hours. My mind is so much clearer now. I don't blame you guys for being angry with me. There are no excuses for what I did, and I won't try to make one. I can only hope you'll give me the opportunity to make it up to you."

Remi didn't have an opportunity to respond before Natalie

cut in, "Here's what we're going to do. If you want to make it up to us, you'll follow this plan without argument. There was an incident with one of the guests last night. Mel will be here sometime today to help decipher some symbols."

"Symbols? What are you talking about?"

"Don't interrupt me," Natalie said harshly.

Richard hung his head, and Remi couldn't help but grin. It was great having a friend who would defend her so strongly, even when she'd let go of the incident herself.

"Depending on how that goes, we may go back to New Orleans with her after Remi takes her midterms."

"Why would we need to go to New Orleans?"

"Was that an argument?"

Richard threw his hands up in mock surrender. "No. Your wish is my command, oh wise one."

Remi giggled.

"Did someone order a research specialist?" a voice called from the doorway leading into the dining room.

"Mel!" Remi squealed and dashed to wrap the woman into a hug. Natalie was right behind her.

"I thought you were coming this afternoon," Natalie laughed. "Sneaky devil."

Mel laughed. "I wanted to see the look on your faces." She gestured toward a man who stood behind her awkwardly in the doorway. "This is Deacon. He works with me at the hotel."

"Hi everyone!" Deacon waved awkwardly.

Richard stepped forward and gave the man a slight nod. "You needed assistance with the invitation?"

Remi was instantly uncomfortable. Richard didn't have to say anything for her to know that he didn't like this guy being in their house.

CHAPTER THIRTY

Mel glanced over her shoulder. "Oh. Well, I asked him to come with me. I figured we might need the extra muscle if things go south. We don't have the team we did last time."

That was true. Their group was considerably larger the last time they battled the curse. Rod, of course, died in the battle and Jamie ran off. They no longer spoke to Brad because he'd betrayed them in the worst way. Baxter was…well, Baxter was Baxter.

"We were about to head to the hotel," Mel told them. "But I wanted to drop by and surprise everyone first. I know Remi probably has a class."

"I do," Remi agreed, but she didn't move for the door.

"Did you already book it?" Natalie asked.

"Not yet."

"Well, then you're staying right here. We had a couple of guests leave last night so there's a room open. One of you can stay there and the other can stay with me and Dani. But I've got to warn you. It's going to be a little unconventional."

"Do you think it's okay? Putting either of them in that room?" Remi asked Natalie.

"Why?" Richard asked.

"I don't see why not," Natalie answered. "It's not any more dangerous than any other room in the house. Plus, it may be better for Mel than photographs."

"Better how?" Richard whined and stomped his foot.

Natalie rolled her eyes. "You better go before you're late for your midterm. I'll get these kids—" she leveled her gaze on Richard, "up to speed."

"Alright. I'll see you guys later." Remi waved and ran for the door.

***

Sophia met Remi outside the classroom. "I was starting to get worried about you."

"It was a crazy night." Remi filled her in on everything that happened the previous day as quickly as she could.

"Holy crap," Sophia raised her eyebrow in a comical way that made Remi laugh.

"Yeah. But our team is mostly back together now. Maybe we can get to the bottom of everything."

"I don't know about her bringing some rando guy."

Remi gave her friend an amused look. "We're a bed & breakfast, Sophia. The house is full of random people on a daily basis."

"I guess you're right about that. Alright, chick. You ready?"

Remi stuffed her phone back in her pocket and threw her shoulders back. "Let's go."

The two girls walked in the classroom. Sophia's phone was clasped in her hand, so that it was well within sight. The professor looked up and narrowed his eyes, but he jerked his head toward a desk in the front row where he'd laid out a test paper for Remi.

Sophia made her way to a desk on the opposite side of the room so that he couldn't later accuse Remi of cheating. "I trust this will be graded fairly," she piped up.

The professor glared at Sophia. "I'm not going to give her a perfect score if she doesn't earn it."

"Of course not," Sophia's tone was cheery, but her meaning was clear, "but you're not going to underscore her because you

CHAPTER THIRTY

didn't get your dick wet."

He growled and looked back at his desk.

Remi picked up her pencil and began the test.

* * *

Two hours later, Remi and Sophia returned to Blackwood Manor. The air was suffocating when they entered the front door. The breath left her body like a punch to the gut. It instantly reminded Remi of the first time she stepped foot in the manor.

Gus gave her a tight smile over his podium.

"What's going on?" Remi asked him.

"Three more customers have complained about…incidents."

Remi groaned. "Were they as bad as the Henderson incident?"

"No, but the last one was really freaked out. Richard's talking to her now."

Natalie entered the foyer with her cell phone held tightly to her ear. She growled and hung up before looking at them. Her gaze fell on Sophia. "So, Sophie. Ever waited tables?"

"Why?" Sophia asked her and gave Remi a confused look.

"I don't know how much Remi has told you, but long story short is we have to keep Richard out of the kitchen for awhile. This means we need to rearrange some jobs. I could use an extra waitress."

Remi's heart soared. It would be great to have another friend in the house watching her back.

"Oh, I don't know," Sophia answered. "I only did it one summer a couple of years back, and I was really bad at it."

"It'll only be for a few weeks at the most," Remi took her friend's hand and gave it a light squeeze. "Just until we can get a replacement. And it won't be like in a restaurant. We only serve meals twice a day. At seven in the morning and six at night. There will only be nine tables at most. Please say you will."

Sophia sighed. "Okay. But you owe me big."

"I know I do." Remi gave Sophia a big, exaggerated kiss on the forehead.

"Really?"

Remi laughed and Natalie cut in.

"Okay, I'm going to go over everything with Sophia real quick."

Remi turned Sophia over to Natalie and headed upstairs. She stopped at the room the Hendersons vacated the night before and knocked before being beckoned inside.

Mel looked up from her place at the desk where she was furiously working on her laptop. A bucket of dirty water sat along the wall and Remi was astounded to see that the walls were furiously scrubbed. There was noticeable discoloration everywhere, but at least they were clean. The room would have to be repainted.

"I'm sorry we had to put you in here under such horrible conditions."

"Oh, honey. Don't worry about it," Mel waved her off. "There were things that didn't show up well in the photos anyway, so it all worked out."

Remi took a seat on the edge of the bed. "What about your friend? I'm sorry I can't remember his name."

CHAPTER THIRTY

"Deacon's staying down the hall in room three." She gave Remi a sympathetic look. "I don't know if anyone's had a chance to tell you more guests left."

Remi nodded. "Gus told me. But he didn't tell me what happened."

"I don't know the details. Natalie said we'd talk about it at dinner tonight."

Remi rose to her feet and turned to the door. "I should probably go introduce myself properly to Deacon."

"You might as well wait for dinner. Natalie's put him to work." Mel chuckled. "She sure hasn't changed."

"She hasn't, but I don't think we'd want her to."

"That's the truth."

They were cut off by Natalie walking in the room without knocking. Both Remi and Mel erupted into a fit of giggles.

"What?" Natalie asked.

Remi waved and put her palms on her knees, willing herself to stop laughing. "Nothing."

Natalie shook her head. "Remi, would you mind taking over the host stand? Gus stayed over to help cover while we got all the staffing situated, but he has an appointment and has to leave now."

"Sure," Remi followed her from the room. "What's everyone doing now?"

"Jessie is going to be doing all the cooking from this point on. Not just dinner. Sophia, Deacon, and I will wait tables. I have Richard doing maintenance on the grounds. You and Gus will have the desk. I moved Joy to cleaning on the day shift."

Joy was a nice older lady they'd hired to work the check-in desk on the day shift. But Remi instantly had a thought that worried her. If Gus had already left for the day, that meant she was on the night shift. She'd already barely slept the night before.

Natalie seemed to sense her apprehension because she put a reassuring hand on her shoulder. "Don't worry. It's just for right now. Gus said he'd come back after his appointment. Tomorrow you'll be on the day shift, and he'll take over his usual nights."

"Excellent," Remi breathed.

"You've been go-go-going, haven't you?" Natalie chuckled. "You didn't tell me about your dirtbag professor."

"I forgot until this morning." That was the truth. The last twenty-four hours were so chaotic that the whole incident was pushed from her mind until she arrived back at the school. Remi's eyes flicked up the stairs. "Do you think I should—"

Natalie shook her head. "Not right now. He's too much of a hothead. Besides, it's been taken care of." Natalie looked through the dining room where Deacon and Sophia were setting the tables for dinner.

Natalie nodded her head. "She's alright."

* * *

Remi didn't have to check-in any new guests, but she did have two cancellations. One provided no explanation, but the other had no issues telling her they were not impressed by the recent reviews, and if they didn't want their business to fail, they'd do well to drop the scare tactics. She sighed when she hung up the phone with that guest. Apparently, the ones that checked out early left nasty reviews. She'd need to check that after dinner. The spreadsheet looked so sad on her computer screen. They'd gone from being completely full for weeks to having four empty rooms. It would be six if Mel and Deacon hadn't shown up. Remi didn't like that. Not one little bit.

Remi rubbed a hand across her tired eyes and glanced toward the sound of the guest floating in from the dining room. She leaned her head back against the wall.

"Just a minute," Remi thought to herself. *"I'll rest my eyes for a minute."*

CHAPTER THIRTY-ONE

Margaret

"Margaret? What's wrong?"

She didn't answer. There wasn't anything she could say. John sighed and rolled back to his side of the bed.

They hadn't made love since he'd come home. It wasn't that she wasn't attracted to him anymore, but every time their interactions started to move in that direction she froze. Images of the soldiers who invaded their home flooded her mind.

John shifted his weight and put his back to the headboard. Margaret rolled to face him. "I'm sorry."

His gaze flitted to hers. "It's starting to feel like you're not in love with me anymore."

Margaret's eyes went wide. "No! Heavens, no! I can't—"

He looked at her. There was a moment where he tried to contemplate what to say, and then he pushed on. "I'm going to ask you a question. I want you to answer me honestly. I promise I won't be mad."

Margaret's heart gave an ominous *thump, thump, thump*. She waited for him to continue.

CHAPTER THIRTY-ONE

"There was something Percy said that got me to thinking. It would explain a lot. He said soldiers came in for a while and that they were mean. He said you haven't been the same since. Margaret, did they—"

Tears slid down her cheeks. They were answer enough.

"Honey, why didn't you tell me?"

"It's so shameful," she wiped away a tear.

"It wasn't your fault. You did what you needed to do to protect our home. You had to know I'd understand that."

She didn't answer as thoughts flew through her mind. It was her fault. It never would have happened if she hadn't engaged in wicked acts with Josie. But she couldn't tell him that.

"That's not where it ended, is it?"

Did Percy tell him about the girl, after all? Did he tell him about that night? The panic must have been evident on her face because he went on to clarify.

"He said something about an altercation. Before the soldiers left?"

Oh. That. She'd forgotten about that after everything that happened. She was thankful that of all her secrets, Percy spilled that one.

"They were here for a long time," she told him. "They came to me and Josie every night. A different one every time. They didn't seem to have any qualms with that. But one night, one of the men caught another going to Lucy's room."

Fury blazed in John's eyes. "She was a baby."

"Three at the time," Margaret confirmed. "He never got a chance to do anything. The man that saw him jumped him and called for the others. They all beat the dickens out of him before hanging him from the banister."

John gave a short snort of laughter. "Well, at least they had limitations. Good riddance to that bastard. Please tell me the children weren't subjected to that?"

Margaret shook her head. "Lucy never woke up. Percy saw the start of the beating, but I told him to go back to his room. I'm surprised he even remembered it."

John breathed a sigh of relief. "Good."

He took her hand and squeezed it. "I would never hold what happened against you. If you hadn't complied, things would have been worse. Look at it this way—it could have been worse. You could have had a baby. Even if you did, we could have figured it out."

Margaret gave him a tight smile and allowed him to pull her into his arms. She looked over his shoulder with a vacant expression on her face.

CHAPTER THIRTY-TWO

Remi

"Remi? Remi," Richard gently shook her.

Remi's eyes snapped open. She was still in her seat at check-in. Barely. She'd half slid off.

She surveyed her surroundings. There wasn't anyone in the immediate vicinity, but the sounds of voices and clinging plates no longer carried from the dining room.

"Did anyone see?"

"I don't know," he shrugged. "You were like that when I came in. They texted me that the guests are done, and they're setting up dinner for us in the kitchen."

So, the guests saw her. Remi flushed with embarrassment. She couldn't even imagine trying to face them later. She rose from her seat and made sure the "ring for service" bell was sitting out before following her husband into the kitchen.

Sophia hugged her when she walked in the room. "I'm so sorry, Remi but I have to go. I'll see you in the morning, okay?"

Remi didn't even have a chance to respond before she rushed from the room. "What's her hurry?"

Natalie gave her a sympathetic smile as she finished setting the table. "A guest yelled at her. She barely got through service. She'll adjust."

"Oh, no." Richard crossed his arms in front of him. "Who was it? I won't have anyone abusing the staff."

"Settle down. The situation has been dealt with. She did make a mistake, but it's been handled."

Richard slammed into a seat. "I don't like it."

"Well, you don't have to like it. This is going to be an adjustment period for everyone, and we have to roll with it."

He opened his mouth to answer when Mel and Deacon entered from the servant's staircase.

"Oh, everything smells so good!" Mel beamed at Jessie who awkwardly blushed.

"Thanks. It's really not a big deal."

"I beg to differ," Natalie told her as they took their seats. "You're literally saving our butts taking on all the kitchen duties. It's not easy when the one person with an open schedule can't go in the kitchen."

"Oh, geez!" Richard looked at Mel and gestured toward Natalie. "Did she tell you why I'm not allowed in here alone?"

Mel nodded. "She did, and I agree with her."

"Not you too!"

"I'm not angry at you, Richard," she told him. "But until we know why that's happening, it's best you avoid it."

Richard turned his gaze to Deacon and narrowed his eyes. "I suppose you think I'm crazy."

The man smiled reassuringly. "Not at all. I'm no stranger to ghosts. I work at Hotel Dahlia, of course."

Richard nodded. "Of course."

"Are you alright?" Jessie asked.

Remi studied Deacon then, and she had to admit that his

color was slightly off.

"I'm okay. My stomach's a little upset."

"It's the nausea," Mel shook her fork and took a sip of water. "The energy here can be a bit overwhelming until you get used to it. It's not as bad as before though."

"Hey guys!" Gus stuck his head in the room. "I wanted to let you know I'm back."

"Are you hungry?" Remi asked.

"No. I grabbed something on the way back. I figure that it's better to not leave the desk unattended for too long. Given the current state of things."

"You're probably right. Thanks, Gus." Natalie said before he disappeared from sight. She turned back to Mel. "Have you learned anything about the symbols yet?"

Mel shook her head and took a sip of water. "Not yet. There's a lot to decipher. I've got a few phrases but not nearly everything."

"Anything you want to share?" Remi chuckled nervously. *Now, why'd I say that?* She wondered to herself. Part of her wanted to bolt from the room, but a bigger part of her wanted to know the truth.

Mel's eyes flickered to Emily, who was distracted by her macaroni and cheese. She gestured for everyone to lean in, and then whispered, "One is *'stay and die,'* another one is, *'Let me run, oh lord.'*"

Richard gave Remi a strange look before turning back to Mel. "That sounds almost contradictory. Like one is a threat and the other is scared."

Mel nodded her agreement. "It'll be hard to tell until I finish all the translations, but I think these symbols were left by two different spirits."

Natalie shook her head. "I went over every square inch of that room. I only picked up on the one dark mass."

"Maybe the other one wasn't dark," Jessie suggested. "Or it was hiding."

"That wouldn't matter," Natalie insisted. "If there was another spirit involved in drawing the symbols, in any way, I would have seen them."

"Well," Richard said cautiously, "you've been unable to see everything before."

Natalie's jaw dropped open as if to protest, but then she closed it. He was right. When she'd snuck into Heaven's Estate, her sight had showed her an empty room and corridor, only to be immediately discovered. She never learned why that happened.

"So, Mel," Remi said brightly, hoping that her unease didn't show in her voice, "how have you been? I know Natalie said you went back to Hotel Dahlia?"

Mel took a bite and swallowed her food before continuing. "I went back a little over a year ago. Cindy called me."

"I thought you two hadn't talked in a while," Richard said.

"We hadn't," Mel agreed. "We had a falling out a long time ago. I didn't even realize she'd gone back to the hotel until she called me. She'd started having some trouble there, and somehow she'd found out about my work here. She thought I might be able to help."

Jessie laughed and everyone turned to look at her. She blushed and looked back to her plate. "Well, it's ironic, right? We're famous in New Orleans."

Collectively, everyone laughed, and Remi couldn't help but smile. Jessie had a point. Who would have thought that Blackwood Manor would be a topic of any kind of

CHAPTER THIRTY-TWO

conversation in a place like New Orleans?

An author had come to visit a while back because she wanted to write a book loosely based on Blackwood Manor. She didn't even use the real name, but everyone in Georgia knew which plantation it was about. The book must've gained traction in New Orleans as well. It was strangely satisfying.

"So, what's going on there?" Richard asked. "You said the place was dormant when you were kids."

Mel shook her head. "Not dormant. Friendly. We saw stuff every day but never felt threatened. It was very different from here. It was more like watching images of a person's life. Most of the time, they didn't even seem aware we were around."

Natalie nodded. No one understood that feeling better than her. She'd often described her gift as a feeling very similar to that. Like watching a movie.

"But I'm guessing things have changed?"

"They have. Things have been steadily building, and we don't have any idea why. Only that it seemed to start getting worse after one particular guest checked out."

"Who was it?" Jessie asked.

"Thurston James. Savy businessman. He owns several restaurant chains in the area. Cindy said she was surprised when he checked in. Hotel Dahlia isn't a dump, but it's not exactly a five-star hotel either. A man of his caliber would typically go for something fancier. Turns out he was extremely demanding and abusive toward the staff. She asked him to leave. He yelled at her that it wasn't over when he made his exit."

Natalie gave Remi a knowing smile. "It kind of sounds like good old Mr. Henderson last night."

Remi disagreed. "No. Yes, he was upset and yelling his head

off, but I couldn't blame him. He woke up to drawings all over his walls and a terrified wife. He was perfectly fine before that point and didn't make any outrageous demands."

"So, Deacon," Richard said, looking at the other man from across the table. "How long have you been at Hotel Dahlia?"

"Oh," Deacon jumped in his chair slightly, almost as if he was surprised to be included in the conversation. "I don't know. Feels like forever. Around two years, I guess."

"How'd you hear about the job?"

Mel chuckled slightly. "Richard, come on. You can't expect him to remember that after so long."

"No, no. It's alright," Deacon waved her off. "There was an ad in the paper. Cindy was desperate for help and took me on right away."

"The hauntings didn't put you off?"

Deacon grinned, leaned back in his chair slightly, and leveled Richard with a knowing look. "Did the hauntings turn you off this place?"

"Not me personally. But I had a score to settle. It wasn't until we managed to clear some of the negative energy from this place that people started coming around. Before that, everyone avoided it like the plague. So, yeah. I guess I'm wondering what would possess someone to go work for a building that has a reputation."

"Richard," Remi hissed and elbowed her husband. She couldn't believe how rude he was being.

Deacon only shrugged. "I think all these old buildings have a history and a spirit or two. It doesn't do any good to be scared of them. After all, they were human beings once, too."

Jessie cleared her throat and turned her focus back to Mel. "So, Richard told me that he asked you to look for the Huangs.

CHAPTER THIRTY-TWO

Any luck?"

Remi dropped her fork and glared at Richard. "Natalie and I both told you we don't believe they had anything to do with that CPS call. Why bring them any more attention?"

"I know, honey. I want to talk to the man. There's no harm in that, right?" he turned to Mel. "Did you find anything?"

"They're staying at a hotel in Savannah."

Remi didn't know how to feel about that information. She didn't like that they were still in Georgia, but it gave weight to her father's story about being here for business.

"What about Jamie?" Natalie asked. "Any luck there?"

Mel sighed. "That's a lot harder. It's like chasing a ghost. She was in Virginia last year. Worked for four months at a hotel before she got fired. Then spent another two at a nearby pancake house. Didn't renew the lease on the crappy apartment she was staying in. I haven't been able to find anything since. Don't worry. I'm still looking."

"What about social media?" Remi asked. "She'd be, what, nineteen now?" Weren't all kids that age obsessed with social media?

"Already looked. Apart from one photo on MemoryBook from before she lived here, there is absolutely nothing."

Natalie ran a hand across her eyes. "This is nuts. She didn't disappear into a puff of smoke."

* * *

"I don't trust him, Remi," Richard told her that night as they got ready for bed. "I felt like he was taunting me."

"We were all sitting around the same table and the only one being an asshole was you," she shot at him. "He came here to help us, and you were ridiculously rude."

"Who asked for his help?" Richard growled. "We don't know anything about this guy. We wanted Mel. To be honest, I'm a little annoyed she brought him here without asking if it was okay."

"Why wouldn't she think it was okay? We welcomed her the first time she came with a group of strangers. And we have strangers in our home every day. Besides, I don't know what the problem is. He's a perfectly nice guy."

Richard shook his head. "There's something about him. I can't put my finger on it."

Remi sighed and crawled between the sheets. "I'm tired, Richard. Can we please go to bed?"

CHAPTER THIRTY-THREE

Margaret

"Margaret? Come here. Don't you want to hold the baby?"

Margaret sat awkwardly in a chair in the corner of the room. John held out his arms and gestured for her to walk forward to where Percy and his wife sat on a couch. They'd just had their first baby, and Margaret's emotions were all over the place. There hadn't been a baby in the house since—well, a long time.

Watching the tiny, wriggling baby from safely across the room was enjoyable. His cries were music to her ears. But she couldn't stop thinking about her behavior when the last baby was here.

John stretched toward her more insistently. She had no choice but to get up and go to them. She nervously looked down into the baby's eyes. His eyes were black as night.

She gasped and shoved the baby at her daughter-in-law before stepping backward.

"Margaret?" John asked, alarmed. "What's wrong?"

"I feel faint," she told him. It was the only excuse that may be plausible for shoving the baby away from her.

Percy stood up and gestured for John to take his spot on the sofa. "Here, Father. You spend some time with the baby. I'll see to Mother."

He took her arm and guided her out of the room. Once he'd sat her in a chair in the kitchen and got her a glass of water, he looked into her eyes. "What really happened in there?"

Margaret knew when she looked into her son's eyes that there was no point in lying to him. She chose to say nothing at all.

"Mother," he said sharply. "I swear to God. If you lay one hand on my family—"

She gasped. "I would never!"

"Wouldn't you?"

It felt like he'd slapped her. They'd never discussed it. Not once in all these years. She'd eventually convinced herself that he'd forgotten all about it. He'd never told anyone. But now, she realized this was why they'd grown apart. This was why he resented her very existence.

She took a deep breath and forced herself not to look away from his hateful stare. "It wasn't like you thought. It wasn't me."

"It wasn't? It sure as hell looked like you."

"It was something in the house. Something made me do those things. It felt real, but it wasn't. I'd give anything to take it back. I can't. But the good thing is, I know the signs now. When I looked at the baby just now, it was like with the girl—"

"Gloria," he growled. "Her name was Gloria. You brought her life, and you took it. At least have the decency to say it."

Margaret swallowed a gulp of water down her dry throat. "It's like it was with—Gloria—his eyes were black, and—"

CHAPTER THIRTY-THREE

He roughly grabbed her by the arms, causing her to cry out. His fingers dug into her arms so hard it hurt. "Are you threatening me?"

"No! I'm trying to—"

He shook her. "You listen to me, god damn it, don't you go spouting that nonsense about my baby being evil. I won't have it! If you lay one hand on him, I will take a fireplace poker and do to you what you did to her! Like I should have done then! Do you understand me? Do you understand?"

"Percy?"

They both looked to the doorway where John stood with a confused expression on his face.

Percy released her and stepped back. Margaret sobbed and instinctively rubbed her arms where he'd gripped them.

John took a step toward his son. "How dare you put your hands on your mother in that manner?"

"John," Margaret darted from her seat to stand between her husband and her son. "Don't. It's not his fault."

"It's not?"

"No. It—"

She glanced back at Percy, whose icy stare slightly thawed. Would he forgive her if she came clean? Is that what it would take for him to realize she wasn't that person anymore?

Margaret turned back to John and took a deep breath. "There's something we need to tell you."

John sat in a chair in the parlor, facing the fireplace. He held his head in his hands. Margaret sat on the floor with her back to the wall. They'd been sitting there in silence for a while.

"Please say something."

He looked up, and his bloodshot eyes filled her with sadness. "Our girl is in there?"

After he'd walked in on her and Percy in the kitchen, they'd told him everything. He hadn't yelled, hadn't screamed. He'd walked straight to the parlor and sat in front of the fireplace. Percy took his wife and baby to Heaven's Estate to visit and give the two of them time to talk.

"Yes," she told him softly.

"Jesus, Margaret," he leaned back in his chair. "You left her in the house?"

"I wasn't in my right mind, John," she said. "It's no excuse. I know that. There is no excuse for what I did. I lost my mind for a while. I was gone. At that time, I wanted her close to me. By the time I realized how twisted it was, I couldn't change it."

"You killed children, Margaret. Children."

This was exactly what she'd been afraid of. She'd known he'd look at her differently, but she hadn't been prepared for the look of disgust on his face.

John was always somewhat weak where children were concerned. When Lucy and Percy were babies, he'd melt into a puddle of cuteness at their every whim.

Margaret leaned forward. "I promise you. Lucy was an accident. I didn't know it was her. As far as the other one goes—I don't know how to explain it. I thought she was evil."

"A child?"

"I know how it sounds. That's why I say I lost my mind. I'd hear voices in my head telling me she was evil. Then unexplainable things would happen, and someone had to be held responsible. Lucy would do wicked things and say a girl told her to. I thought it was the little one. That's what I called her. The girl. I never named her."

"Percy said her name was Gloria."

"That's what Josie called her. To me she was, "the girl."

CHAPTER THIRTY-THREE

"You're not making a strong case for yourself, Margaret."

"I know. But I need to be honest."

"Honest?" he spat. "You've been dishonest ever since the war ended."

"I know. I need you to understand, though. The moment it was all done, I was horrified with myself. When I realized what I'd done— I thought about taking my own life. I would have if Percy wasn't here. It was never my intention to kill them."

"If it wasn't your intention, why the hell did you go down to the cellar with a gun in the first place?"

"Again, I'd lost my mind. I thought I had no choice. I was convinced you were coming home, and you'd punish me when you found the evil child in the home. I never intended to end her. If that's what I wanted, I would have drowned her at birth. I wanted to get the demon out of her. I thought I could save her."

"This is insane."

"That's what I'm telling you. I agree."

"Alright, Margaret. Here's what's going to happen." He leaned forward to look her in the eye. "I'm not going to draw attention to this. It would be an embarrassment to our family, and I won't put that boy through any more than you already have. Outside the home, we will present a unified front and be a happy family. But at home, we are nothing. We will sleep in separate bedrooms. I want nothing to do with you. I better not ever see you touch that child again. Do you understand me?"

She nodded. "Yes. I don't want to. I don't trust myself."

"That's a good thing. Because no one else does, either. Now, I'm going to move my things to another room. I can't stand the sight of you."

He got to his feet and left her sobbing on the floor of the parlor.

CHAPTER THIRTY-FOUR

Margaret

Margaret moved through the next several years of her life in a blur. Her marriage to John was now a front. He'd been true to his word the night he'd learned the truth. She'd hoped that once the sting of everything settled, he would become affectionate again, but she was wrong.

When they were at a social function, she could pretend things were the way they used to be. He'd hold her and look at her lovingly. He even kissed her forehead sometimes. Those moments were very real for Margaret, and she cherished them.

At home, though, things were very different. They took their meals separately, they slept separately, and if they did come across each other in the hallway they didn't speak.

John eventually brought in more servants to help get the house back to running the way it used to. She saw the curious stares and exchanged glances between them, but she was past the point of caring.

Holidays were a particular torture for her. Though they had the bigger home, John always went to spend holidays with Percy and his family. She wasn't invited unless someone important was supposed to be there. On the rare occasion she did go, she took great care not to touch her grandchildren. It was harder than she'd originally imagined. They were beautiful children. Robert was growing up to be a handsome young man, and she never saw the black eyes on him again. And the girl, Madeleine, looked so much like Lucy. It made her heart ache every time she saw her.

When they'd been small children, Robert and Madeleine would run toward her, lifting their chubby arms and wanting to be held, but she'd darted to hide behind John. Now, they no longer tried.

Margaret sometimes sobbed over the irony. One night and one decision shaped the course of her life into this ugly, monstrous thing it now was.

"May I be blunt, Miss Margaret?" Josie's voice tore her out of one of her stupors one night. She'd been sitting on the porch crying, and her old friend sat next to her on the steps. Margaret yelped and whipped to the side in disbelief. No. It couldn't be Josie. Josie was dead, and Margaret killed her.

Josie looked over at her, and Margaret was astonished to see that she didn't have a face. It was as though a thin curtain were pulled tightly over her face. There were impressions for her eyes and lips, as though they lay under the surface, and yet they weren't there.

"No," Margaret muttered and wiped the tears from her cheeks. "No, you're not here."

"But I am. I've always been here."

"Did you not have the chance to pass over?"

"I did," Josie admitted. "But I lost my chance."

"Why?"

CHAPTER THIRTY-FOUR

"I couldn't leave her."

"She's still here because I didn't baptize her?"

"Don't you blame yourself for that. Those girls were in so much shock by what happened that it took time for them to work out they weren't alive anymore. By that time, they'd missed the window. I wouldn't leave Gloria. She's too fragile and unable to navigate this world. I don't worry about Miss Lucy. She's adjusted quite nicely."

"She's okay?"

"She plays with the others every day. Quite the social butterfly."

"Others?"

"Miss Margaret," Josie's tone had a teasing lilt to it, "surely, you didn't think we were the only ones. You said it yourself. You don't have those wicked thoughts anymore. Who do you think was making you see those things?"

"I thought I went crazy."

"Crazy because of what they showed you. Funny how those thoughts went away after that night."

"Except for when Robert was born. It was only the one time though. I swear it."

Josie shook her head. "Not even then. You never acted on it. Because you acknowledged it was a hallucination. That's more than you did back then."

"Robert," Margaret whispered and sunk her head into her hands. "I've made a mess of everything, Josie. My entire family hates me. I can't understand it. There was a time I did. But enough time has passed now, can't they see that I'm not like that? I can't touch my own grandchildren. John and Percy both threatened me with bodily harm if I ever did. What can I do to make them see? I'm not like that, Josie. You know I'm not."

"They may see you more favorably if you assist the girls now."

"How can I do that?"

"Can you think of nothing?"

She honestly couldn't.

Josie sighed. "Do you recall telling me about a strange dream you had when you were pregnant with Gloria? The woman who told you that one of your children was destined to end evil?"

"Oh." Margaret hadn't thought about that in so long. "The one that told me to protect them at all costs? That something would play with my mind—"

Margaret squeezed her eyes shut as the realization hit her. That hadn't been a dream. It was a prophecy. She'd been told exactly what would happen and played right into evil's hands anyway.

"Yes, ma'am," Josie said.

"I'm such a fool," Margaret whispered. "Which one was it?"

"It could be either one, I suppose," Josie told her. "I see qualities in them both, but my gut tells me it was Gloria. She's the one the house was turning you against."

Margaret could see that. From the day of the child's birth, something played with her mind. "I don't see what I can do about it now."

"You may still be able to help her," Josie told her. "It's come to my attention over the years that the land has been cursed by an evil magic. One of the girls had the ability to vanquish it, so the house needed to eliminate them before they were old enough to realize their power."

"How does this help now?"

CHAPTER THIRTY-FOUR

"There is a stone made by a good witch that, in the right hands, can end the evil. I don't know for certain, but as their mother, it may work for you. If you succeed, you can open the doorway again for them to pass."

"Of course I'll try. Where is this stone?"

"Under a loose floorboard in the servant's quarters."

Josie's image began to flicker in and out of focus.

Then she was gone.

Margaret gathered her skirts and made her way to the servants' quarters. She didn't knock when she entered, and one of the maids jumped.

"I'm sorry, Miss Margaret. You startled me. Can I help you with anything?"

"Could you place new sheets on my bed?"

The girl turned slightly to the side, and her eyes narrowed.

"For Heaven's sake!" Margaret thought to herself. *"Go away!"*

"Yes, ma'am. Of course." The girl finally curtsied and scurried from the cottage.

Margaret paused for a moment to make sure she was gone before beginning her search. She walked around slowly, making sure to distribute her weight on each board. She was about to give up when one squeaked underfoot.

Margaret knelt to the ground and easily pried the board up. She saw an old book covered in cobwebs and slid it to the side. Underneath the book was a beautiful blue stone. She pulled it out and held it in her hand. She didn't know what she expected, but nothing happened. It was a rock. Very beautiful. But still a rock. Still, Josie wouldn't have told her it was there if it wasn't important.

She heard footsteps crunching in the grass outside and hurriedly slid the floorboard back into place. Keeping the stone grasped tightly in her hand, she left the cottage.

* * *

Margaret tried to make sense of the blue stone for months. She couldn't understand how she was supposed to use it to help her daughters and win back her family's favor. She didn't know how to use it or even where it came from.

Margaret cried at night and begged Josie to come back and tell her what to do, but she didn't see her friend anymore.

One night, she dreamed of the woman again. She was in that dark, foggy place once again when she saw her. Years had passed, and it showed on Margaret's lined face, but this woman looked the same as she did the last time.

The woman gave her a sad look and shook her head. "I wish you'd listened."

"What's your name?" Margaret asked. She immediately felt foolish. Of all the things to ask this woman, her name seemed the least important.

"My name is Rebecca. But do not deflect. Did I not warn you that your children were needed? That you needed to protect them at all costs?"

A tear streamed down Margaret's face, and the shame rolled through her body like a billion burning embers. "I thought it was a dream."

"A dream can still be based in reality," Rebecca told her simply. "I warned you they would try to trick you to get to the children. I told you not to fall for it. You did anyway."

CHAPTER THIRTY-FOUR

"Is there nothing that can be done?" Margaret asked tearfully. "Josie led me to a stone—"

"Yes, yes. The haven stone. I created it to combat evil."

"So, you're a witch then?"

"Such a nasty term for it, but yes."

"Please tell me what to do. How do I use this stone?"

"Margaret, you can't. That was your children's job."

Margaret's heart plummeted into her stomach. "There's no hope? Percy—"

"The boy is not the one."

"So, we are doomed forever?"

"Eventually, others will come that can fulfill the job. All we can do at this point is wait, and when they come, prepare them to the best of our ability."

When Margaret woke up, the conversation played on repeat in her mind. She could think of nothing else as the hours turned into days, and the days turned into weeks. She couldn't accept that she could do nothing but wait for another generation to do what was Lucy's or Gloria's job. The thought of her girls lying in limbo in the dark, gloomy house tortured her. It was even worse than the realization she'd never make peace with her family. She couldn't be at peace knowing they were still wasting away in the house.

The following morning, Margaret bade her time. She waited until the servants cleaned her bedroom and John was out of the house before shutting herself behind closed doors with the haven stone and sleeping powder that the doctor gave to John.

She took all the powder and lay back against the pillows, closed her eyes, and clasped the stone tightly in her hand.

"You stupid fool!" A harsh voice awakened Margaret. When

she opened her eyes, her surroundings were dark and gloomy.

Josie stood over her, and though she had a veil for a face, she appeared livid. Margaret was taken aback. Josie's tone had never been quite so sharp. Even when everything was happening with Gloria.

"What?" she asked.

"How are you supposed to help them now?"

Margaret furrowed her brows. "What do you mean?"

Then she saw it. She was lying next to a body on her bed. She stared into the face and realization gripped her tightly. It was her own face she was staring into, pale and lifeless.

Margaret shot to her feet and stared harder, willing the image to change. "What?" she whispered again.

She was disturbed by a knock on the bedroom door and one of the servants entering. "Miss Margaret?" she said as she approached the bed.

The girl walked right through Margaret to get there, startling her into stepping back. She checked Margaret's pulse and then her gaze landed on the empty box of powder on the nightstand. She gathered her skirts and ran to the door, yelling for someone to go for the doctor.

"No, no," Margaret protested and pressed herself against the wall. "This can't be happening."

"What did you think would happen?" Josie asked, coldly.

"I thought if I went into a deep enough sleep that the window might open. For you and the girls."

"Well, congratulations. It didn't work, and you've killed yourself."

"No," Margaret protested again. "The maid will bring the doctor. Everything will be fine."

As if in answer to her prayers, there were thundering

CHAPTER THIRTY-FOUR

footsteps down the hall. Three more servants entered the room, along with John and the town doctor. He must have been downstairs to come so quickly. *"Fate."* Margaret thought to herself and smiled. *"It's fate that he was downstairs. He's going to save me."*

The doctor listened to her heart and felt her pulse before looking back up at John. "She's gone."

Margaret's smile fell. "What? No. You didn't even try. Try, damn you!"

John put a hand to his mouth and squeezed his eyes closed.

The doctor's eyes fell on the bedside table and the empty container of sleeping powder. "She took all of it. Why would she do that, John?"

But her husband didn't answer. Instead, he hung his head and walked slowly from the room.

CHAPTER THIRTY-FIVE

Remi

Remi shot straight up in bed and breathed heavily. Her chest ached from the thumping that occurred under the surface. She placed a shaky hand to her chest and forced herself to take short, steady breaths. In and out. In and out.

She glanced next to her and jumped when she saw the form of another body facing the wall. She put a cautious hand on the shoulder when she realized it was only Richard. Richard. Her husband. Not her own cold, dead corpse.

Remi struggled to untie the bells from her wrist and crawled from the bed. When she opened the door, she winced at the sound of the tinkling from the handle. She glanced over her shoulder at her husband who still slept soundly.

Remi walked down the hall toward the servant's stairwell but stopped a few feet short of the door. Her heart began to thunder again, and a chill ran down her spine. *Something's waiting for you in there.* The voice in her head was clear and articulate. She didn't know where it came from, and she didn't care. Instead, she turned and went down the front staircase.

CHAPTER THIRTY-FIVE

She didn't normally go this way for midnight snack runs, but only a couple of the rooms had guests anyway, and she doubted they'd be downstairs at this time of night.

"Remi," Gus looked up with surprise from his place at the host stand. "Are you okay? Did something happen?"

"No." She shook her head and forced herself to smile at him. "I need a little coffee."

"Why are you coming this way?"

She chose to ignore him and head for the kitchen.

"Wait! Why are you going this way?" he called again and ran after her.

"Remi!" Gus said insistently as she started the coffee pot. "What happened?"

"I woke up in my own bed," she said flatly.

"That's great," he said impatiently. "What was the dream about?"

She sighed and leaned against the counter. "I saw how Margaret died."

"Oh shit," he took a seat at the island. "That must have been horrifying."

"No. It was more sad than scary. Her reaction when she realized she was dead—well, I don't think I'll ever forget that."

"So, how'd it happen?"

"Accidental suicide."

"Huh?"

"She took a sleeping medication in powder form. But I don't think she meant to die. She was very upset. I believe she wanted to be close to the edge."

"Why?"

She squeezed her eyes closed. "It's kind of a blur. Something about helping the girls cross over. Maybe Natalie will be able to see the rest of it in the morning."

Remi was about to answer when Lucy suddenly appeared next to her and roughly grabbed her elbow. She dropped her coffee mug and turned to look into the girl's frantic eyes.

"Shit!" Gus exclaimed and rose to his feet.

"You have to come! That man is here. He's going to take Emily!"

Remi's throat seized and she ran for the staircase without stopping to explain to a confused Gus. Luckily, she could hear him following behind her. They turned into the family wing as a figure exited Emily's bedroom.

"STOP!" she screamed.

The figure stopped and turned. The moonlight from the window hit the face, and she could see that it was her father with a sleeping Emily cradled in his arms.

More footsteps joined them in the hallway.

"Sir," she heard Deacon speak with an authoritative tone. "Lay the little girl down on the ground and step away."

"No. She is my granddaughter, and we are leaving this place."

"You aren't going anywhere," Deacon answered and stepped forward slowly. His voice took on a lower register and danger flashed in his eyes momentarily. "I'm going to tell you one more time to put her down and step away."

Malaki laughed. "Or what? You aren't going to do anything to me while I'm holding her." He turned his gaze back to Remi. "I swear, every single person you associate with is an idiot. It's no wonder you turned into one of them."

Lucy materialized behind Malaki, and Remi's breath caught in her throat. The young girl approached him with a menacing look in her eye. It was a look that Remi remembered well from the old days. This was pre-battle Lucy, and she was pissed.

CHAPTER THIRTY-FIVE

Lucy grabbed his arm, and before he could react, she sank her teeth into him. He howled, and his grip loosened on Emily.

Remi watched as, almost as if in slow motion, her daughter fell toward the ground. Gus dove forward and caught her before she hit the floor. Deacon tackled Malaki, but Lucy still clung to his arm, blood running freely from the wound.

"Let go! Let go of me!" Malaki screamed as he struggled to get away from the combined grip of Deacon and Lucy.

"Oh my," a voice said from behind them.

Remi turned to see one of the guests peeking around the corner. "We have caught an intruder. Please go back to your room."

The woman scurried away as if embarrassed she'd been caught snooping, and Remi turned back to the scene in front of her.

"Lucy. Lucy, I've got him. Let go." Deacon said.

The girl listened and leaned back, doing nothing to disguise the blood rolling down her chin.

Deacon pinned Malaki's arms behind his back and jerked him to his feet. "Remi," he called to her, "do you have any rope?"

"There's some in the cellar," she answered, and raced for the steps to retrieve it. She was halfway down when she had a disturbing thought.

Deacon called Lucy by her name. She knew who Lucy was, and she was sure some of the others did too, but how did Deacon? He'd only just arrived.

* * *

An hour later, the house was bustling with activity, and Remi was once again too tired to think straight. Three squad cars showed up, answering the calls of their remaining guests.

When her father was loaded into the backseat of one of them, he'd been screaming about grandparent's rights and calling her an unfit mother.

One officer pulled her to the side to get her version of what happened. She explained honestly about their volatile relationship, and how he'd been kicked out of the house for being disrespectful. She told him about the night she'd found her mother in the nursery without permission.

A quick scan of the house found that Kylie was removed from her crib before they knew Malaki was in the house. One of the officers found her crying softly in a car seat of a car in the parking lot.

Emily never woke up throughout the whole ordeal, so she'd been transported to the hospital to be checked, along with Richard who also never woke up.

Remi desperately wanted to go be with them, but the officers requested she stay behind until they'd finished questioning everyone about what happened.

So, now Remi sat on the bottom step of the staircase waiting. Gus entered from the dining room where one of the officers took him to talk. He sat down next to Remi on the step and took her hand.

"The little girl bit him!" the nosy lady from upstairs exclaimed from her place in the parlor. "Blood was everywhere!"

"The little girl is unconscious, ma'am," the officer calmly told her.

"No. Not her. The other one. The blonde."

"Oh, God," Remi whispered.

CHAPTER THIRTY-FIVE

"It'll be over soon," Gus told her.

They sat there for another moment before he probed her with a serious question. "Why do you think he did it?"

"To make my life miserable?" Remi shrugged. "Who knows? He's been unnecessarily harsh my entire life."

Gus nodded. "Understanding why he wasn't at your wedding."

Remi gave a wry laugh. "You got it. I don't know why, but the man hates me. I've never done one damn thing in my entire life that he approved of. He's saying I'm an unfit mother, but not why he thinks that."

Meow.

The sound caused Remi to jump and jerk around. Whiskers sat two steps up staring down at them. She cocked her little head to the side, as if amused by all the activity that awakened her from her peaceful sleep.

"Whiskers!" Remi sighed and put a hand to her chest. "You scared the living daylights out of me, cat."

Meow.

Whiskers jumped into her lap and rubbed her head against Remi's chest. Instantly, she felt calm wash over her.

Gus looked down at the cat and back at Remi with an amused grin. "I never asked. Why'd you name her Whiskers?"

"What?"

"Whiskers. Why'd you name her that? That's a name you'd expect a kid to come up with. I would have expected you to come up with something really sophisticated."

"Oh. I don't know," Remi tried to think back. It was a fair question, and it was one she'd never thought about before. "I never thought about it. That was her name. It was almost like she chose it."

"Mrs. Price?" The officers regrouped in the foyer and Remi and Gus got to their feet to be eye level with them. "We've gathered everyone's statements, and we'll let you be for the night."

"Thank you," she told them.

"I'm guessing you want to press charges?"

"Damn right. Do I need to come down tonight though? I really want to go check on the girls and my husband."

"You can come down in the morning. We'll be there."

The officers said goodbye and left. Once they were gone, the nosy woman from earlier turned her gaze on Remi. "I want my money back."

Remi sighed. Of course she did.

"You go on." Gus gave her shoulder a reassuring squeeze. "I'll take care of it."

* * *

When Remi entered the hospital room an hour later, her heart soared. Richard sat up in the bed and cradled Kylie in his arms. He smiled at her.

"Hey, there's Mama," he whispered in the sweet baby's ear. "She's getting hungry." He grinned.

"Poor thing," Remi strode forward and took Kylie from him. She settled into the armchair next to the bed and pulled out her breast to feed the squirming baby.

Remi nodded toward Emily who lay curled into Richard's side with her head on his chest. "How's she doing?"

CHAPTER THIRTY-FIVE

"We're all fine," Richard reassured her. "Once they checked us over and determined we were all fine, they let us all in the same room."

"So, what was it?"

"It's weird," Richard shook his head. "I wasn't drugged. I woke up in the ambulance on the way here and totally freaked out. I had no clue what was going on. The paramedic told me what happened." He scowled. "I should have listened to you when you told me what kind of man he was. I'm sorry, babe."

"It's not your fault," Remi said softly.

"If I hadn't let him stay—"

"It would have happened sooner."

Emily whimpered slightly. Remi looked at her and sighed. "I can't believe she slept through it."

"She woke up a little when we first got here. Then passed right back out. She doesn't remember anything."

"Thank God," Remi leaned her head back against the chair. "I've been worried she was traumatized."

"We got lucky there. She's sleeping deeper than she does at home."

"Well, she's been sleep deprived. If only we could all sleep it off. But they'll probably be letting you guys go soon."

Richard nodded. "We're waiting for one test. But the doctor didn't seem too concerned. How'd you know? What was going on? They said Kylie had already been removed from the house."

"Believe it or not, Lucy told me. She even helped to stop him."

Richard's eyes widened. "Lucy? Lucy Blackwood?"

"She's taken a liking to Emily. She's not too bad."

Richard raised an eyebrow.

"Really," Remi insisted. "I think we got rid of whatever made her vicious before. Now she's like she was in life. Now, she's our daughter's friend. She just happens to be dead."

Richard shook his head. "I don't understand how that's even possible. I mean, how can they be a dark spirit, and then suddenly not?"

"I'm not sure exactly how it works. I think it has something to do with the haven stone. The energy levels."

"Well, we'll figure it out." Richard smiled at her.

She grinned back. "I know we will."

She closed her eyes.

CHAPTER THIRTY-SIX

Margaret

"Why did the light never appear for me?" Margaret asked Josie one day when they lounged in the parlor. Josie looked at her as if she'd grown an extra limb. "What?"

"I would have thought that's obvious. You killed people, Margaret. Then you killed yourself. You took four lives."

"I didn't intend to."

Josie laughed. "Yes, you did. You may have been influenced into believing things that weren't true, but you still made a conscious decision. You have to be held responsible. It's that simple."

A few weeks passed since Margaret's death, and she was still grappling with how her new existence worked. In many ways, it was a blessing having her old friend here to guide her through. Sometimes though, like now, it was obvious Josie still held resentment toward her.

The afterlife wasn't what Margaret always imagined at all. She couldn't leave Blackwood Manor, and she'd tried. She'd thought it would be a good opportunity to find her sister, whom she hadn't seen since she married John. She also wanted to find Beau and thank him for everything he did to help her that night, but she hadn't seen him since the following week after he'd finished with the fireplace. She'd been unable to go past the tree lined path in the front, or past the cemetery in the back.

The first time she tried, she felt a strange tingling course through her body. The second time, she'd been thrown bodily back several feet. She'd pounded the ground and screamed at the top of her lungs.

"Do you think I'd still be here if it was that simple?" Josie asked her when she'd complained about it.

"But it is possible?" Margaret asked her hopefully.

Josie shrugged. "In all these years, I've only known of one who was able to come and go as they wished. He hasn't been back in several years. I don't know if he ended up crossing over, or if he figured out how to have a life away from here. We'll probably never know."

This was hardly good news in Margaret's eyes. She'd grown up being told all about guardian angels, and that when her time came, she'd be able to look over her loved ones. It was all a lie. She'd be able to watch over John, as long as he remained in the house, but she couldn't even go a few miles down the road to check on her son and grandchildren. It was a travesty.

She was also frustrated when she looked around and saw what the others could do. Some of them moved items around. One of the men liked to be fresh when the living maids would walk by.

The biggest shock for Margaret was the various appearances of the different spirits. Some of them had horns and blue scaly skin. Her first thought was they were demons, but Josie shot that theory down. "They're not demons. They aren't good people. Every bad act chips away at our souls and can change the way we physically look. Mostly if we harm someone. But even interfering with the living can mean a visual punishment."

"Is that why?" Margaret gestured to Josie's face, unable to bring herself to say the words."

"One of the others told me I look like this because my face was destroyed before my heart stopped beating."

Margaret felt immediate shame at her role in that scenario. "Well, I guess I'll look like this forever," she'd said instead. "I couldn't interfere with the living if I tried."

Josie tilted her head to the side. "It's only been a matter of weeks. You'll be able to eventually. We all have the power. But it's a skill you have to learn like any other. We can show ourselves at any moment, but we choose not to."

"Why?"

"What's the point? If we have negative repercussions when it does happen, it's not worth it. Things do happen accidentally. We can be startled like the living. Accidents are less likely to get us in trouble. And special circumstances are sometimes taken into consideration, but for the most part, we're to leave it alone. Otherwise, we make ourselves her target. You don't want that."

Just who *her* was, Margaret didn't ask. It never occurred to her to ask who she could potentially be in trouble with. Maybe it was from being the mistress of Blackwood Manor for so long, but it was inconceivable to her that she'd need to answer to anyone.

Despite Josie's assurances, Margaret went years without being able to have any control over any kind of powers. She couldn't move things like the others, she couldn't talk to residents.

The first time she felt like there was any hope was when the house got a new maid. The woman walked through the door, and her energy was different. There was something different about her the minute Margaret laid eyes on her, and somehow, she felt it was mutual. But she couldn't be sure.

A couple of weeks later, she knew she was right. She was standing in the kitchen when the maid entered. The woman gasped, clutched the laundry she carried tight to her chest, and ran back out of the room.

Did she see me? Margaret wondered. *Yes, she definitely saw me. But why?*

Before she could piece together why, a pain tore through her very core. She didn't even know the last time she'd experienced pain. Definitely when she'd been alive. It hurt so terribly. When the wave finally passed, and she looked down, she saw that her feet were replaced with hooves.

"That woman is a Seer," Josie told her when she saw the hooves. "You must stay clear of her. She's dangerous to our kind."

"What is a Seer?"

"A living person with the ability to intermingle with our world."

"How is that bad?"

"We can interfere without meaning to. You must avoid her to the best of your ability."

Margaret nodded, but she had no intention of heeding her friend's warning. If this one truly was a Seer, she could be the answer to getting Margaret out of this nightmare.

CHAPTER THIRTY-SEVEN

Remi

"Remi? Wake up, babe," Richard's voice roused her from sleep.

She didn't know how long she'd been out, but Remi couldn't deny it was the best sleep she'd gotten in a while.

"Sorry to have to wake you," Richard gave her a regretful smile. "You looked so peaceful. But the doctor said we can go."

The hospital room came back into view. Kylie slept soundly against her breast, and Emily was still knocked out in the hospital bed.

Remi carefully rearranged her shirt to make sure her breast was covered and stood up, carefully cradling Kylie.

Richard scooped up Emily in his arms and grabbed their discharge paperwork.

"I'll drive," he told her as they placed the girls in their car seats.

Remi didn't argue. She tossed him the keys and slipped into the passenger seat. She was grateful for the reprieve. The nap in the hospital was nice, but she was sure she shouldn't be behind the wheel yet. She glanced at the clock on the dashboard and groaned.

"What's wrong?" Richard asked.

"I'm supposed to be on day shift at the desk. Gus should have gone home an hour ago. We're lucky he's so dedicated."

"I'll take the day shift. You go to bed."

"I'm pretty sure Natalie will have a problem with that."

Richard shrugged. "It's not Natalie's house."

"Can I please be there when you tell her that?"

Richard gave her an amused grin. "Natalie's biggest gripe is me being in the kitchen. For obvious reasons. The front desk isn't in the kitchen. I think we'll be okay."

Remi looked out her window at the passing scenery and hoped he was right.

* * *

Natalie was already there when they walked in the front door. She immediately wrapped Remi in a tight hug, then pulled back and looked deep into her eyes. The question lingered between them like fog and Remi nodded.

Natalie stepped back and allowed Remi to step forward to look around her. Gus was no longer at the desk.

"I sent him home," Natalie said. "He hasn't gotten much more sleep than you have recently."

"That's the truth," Remi sighed. "Richard wants me to go to sleep, and he'll take over the day shift."

"Absolutely not."

CHAPTER THIRTY-SEVEN

"Oh for the love of God," Richard snapped. "The woman needs sleep."

"I agree," Natalie said. "But it's too easy for you to slip into the kitchen alone if you're at the desk."

"I'm not going to."

Natalie's eyes softened slightly. "I wish we could believe you. But you have to earn that trust back."

"Fine," he spat through clenched teeth and stomped up the stairs.

Remi felt bad for her husband. She knew that the lack of trust would be affecting him deeply, but she had to agree with Natalie. It hadn't been that long since he'd succumbed to the bottle all over again. It hadn't been long since he'd slapped her so hard across the face that she'd fallen to the ground.

Remi gave her friend an apologetic smile. "I don't think I can stay awake through the shift."

"I wouldn't expect you to." Before she said another word, Natalie's girlfriend Dani entered from the parlor.

"Hey, Remi."

"Hey, Dani," Remi raised an eyebrow at Natalie.

"I asked her to help out today. It's her day off at the restaurant."

Remi nodded. She'd never worked with Dani before, but she didn't have any reason not to trust her. She'd been with Natalie for years, and if she trusted her, so did Remi.

"I'm going to grab a glass of water and head on up," Remi told them before heading for the kitchen.

She grabbed a glass from the cabinet and poured a glass. The back door opened, and Deacon walked in. He wore a work shirt and gloves on his hands.

"Oh. Hey," he said in surprise when he noticed her.

"Hey. I never got a chance to thank you for your help last night."

He averted his gaze and walked toward the doorway into the dining room. "Don't mention it. Anyone would have done the same thing."

"Hey, Deacon," she called to him.

He turned in the doorway to look at her. "Yeah?"

"How'd you know her name?"

"What?"

"The girl that bit him. You said, 'Lucy let go. I've got him.' How'd you know her name?"

"You said it."

"I'm pretty sure I didn't."

He didn't answer her. He turned around and speed walked out of the room.

Remi narrowed her eyes and placed her glass in the sink. If anything, her suspicions had been heightened. She made her way to the servant's staircase.

CHAPTER THIRTY-EIGHT

Margaret

"Why can you see me?" Margaret asked.

The maid screamed and twirled around from her place at the sink. The plate she'd been washing slipped through her soapy fingers and hit the floor with a loud crash.

The woman's eyes were wide with fright, and her breathing was ragged.

"Why can you see me?" Margaret asked again.

Now, the woman rolled her eyes and strolled to the walk-in pantry to grab a broom. "Why can't you people leave me alone?"

"So, this has happened before?"

The woman sighed as she knelt to sweep up the remnants of the plate. "All my life."

"Then why did you seem so scared?"

"Because usually you all don't have the gall to approach me," the woman snapped. She tipped her dustpan into the garbage can.

"What's your name?"

"Sadie."

She went back to the sink and continued washing the dishes. Margaret moved around the kitchen island so that Sadie couldn't avoid her.

"Why can you see me?"

"I don't know. They call it a gift. I don't think I'd go that far. I can see the dead, and I can see the essence of living souls through colored auras."

"You can see the dead, but you don't talk to us often?"

"I can't say I ever have. Usually, they go the other way when they notice me."

"Why?"

"Well, it's my understanding that associating with someone like me is harmful to your kind."

Margaret looked down at her hooves and recalled what Josie said about staying as far away from this woman as she could. She chose to ignore it. In all these years, Sadie was the only living person she'd been able to make contact with, and she couldn't ignore such an opportunity.

"You have to help me."

"Why should I?" Sadie laughed. "You've done horrible things."

Fury flooded Margaret, and she had to ball her hands into fists to avoid striking this aggravating woman. She was so tired of one mistake being held over her head. How long would she have to pay for one mistake? She was trying to make things right! Why couldn't anyone understand that?

"Something in this house made me. I can't explain it."

Sadie nodded. "I can see that. There is darkness here. Still, you made choices. I'm afraid I can't cross you over."

"I don't want you to cross me over. I want you to cross the

CHAPTER THIRTY-EIGHT

girls over."

"I can't do that either."

"But they're innocent."

"That doesn't matter," Sadie turned to face her again. "I'm not God. I can't change the way things are."

"So, there's nothing that can be done?"

"There are people in the world who have the power. But I don't personally know any. Usually, these people don't even know they have the power in advance. I can't even begin to guide you on that."

"Sadie!" a voice called out from the opposite side of the house.

"I have to go," Sadie told her, "before you get me fired."

Sadie hadn't even fully left the room before the pain tore through Margaret once again. This time it settled in her head. It was blinding, and she believed for a moment that her head might explode. She screamed and clutched her head. She hadn't thought it was possible, but this pain was even greater than when she'd grown the hooves.

When it finally passed, Margaret sank to the ground. *What happened to me?* She looked up and Josie stood across the room.

"What did you do?" There was no anger or malice in the other woman's voice. Only a sorrow that Margaret could not understand.

"The pain—" She couldn't find the words to explain what she'd experienced.

"Go look in a mirror," Josie told her.

Margaret got to shaky feet and walked into the dining room. The current owners had a large, ornate mirror hanging over a liquor cabinet. Her hands flew to her mouth in shock at the image that stared back at her.

Her skin was now blue, and horns grew out of her forehead in large, long spikes. The skin surrounding the base was red, as if it bled. Thankfully, her hands and face were still recognizable despite the blue color.

"You can't listen? Even now?" Josie's regretful voice spoke from behind her.

Margaret turned to face her old friend. Anger consumed her very essence when she finally realized she was on her own.

CHAPTER THIRTY-NINE

Remi

Remi tapped her foot furiously against the floor. She sat on the edge of her bed chewing her lip and tap, tap, tapping away. She'd only slept a few minutes.

It got to the point recently where her insomnia was her new normal, and sleep was this strange, outlandish thing that felt like a fairy tale.

She didn't want the others to know she was awake already, so she continued to sit. She didn't need the looks. Natalie was great, she was concerned for her mental health with being so sleep deprived. She knew that the others thought she was cracking up. It was obvious in the sideways glances and exchanged looks when they didn't think she could see. It hurt. She considered all these people here friends, and she couldn't believe that they thought she was losing her mind.

Remi slid back in the bed and rested her back against the headboard. She let her thoughts consume her. Hurt and anger flowed through her veins, and she allowed the tears to fall from her eyes.

What more did she have to do to convince people she was a

good person?

Go to sleep, Remi. You need your sleep, Remi. Get some rest, Remi. All that thinly veiled "concern" was maddening. Just a fancy, polite way of telling her that she was insane.

The baby monitor crackled to life on the bedside table, and Kylie's cries filled the room.

Remi covered her ears and let out a strangled cry. The tears flowed harder down her face. Those cries. Those persistent cries. They were the reason why she couldn't sleep. If everyone was so concerned about her lack of sleep, why weren't they helping her?

She squeezed her hands tighter over her ears, but Kylie's cries got louder and louder.

Fine, she snapped to herself and threw herself out of the bed and across the floor. She was nearly to the nursery when an even louder cry called out from the opposite side of the hallway. Remi threw open the door to Emily's bedroom and stared at her daughter.

The girl lay with her back flat on the mattress. She kicked her legs and swung her arms, screaming at the top of her lungs. Her cheeks were bright red from the force of her screams.

Lucy sat next to her bed, trying to whisper calm assurances into the girl's ear, but she screamed louder. Lucy looked at Remi apologetically. "I only left the room for a minute. When I came back, she was upset. I don't know what happened."

Remi knew what happened. Her daughter was having another tantrum over sleep, and enough was enough.

"Emily. Stop that! Big girls don't act like that."

Emily stopped swinging her limbs, but she continued to scream. Remi's nerves were shot. She couldn't take it anymore. Cloudiness covered her vision from the inside. She felt as if

CHAPTER THIRTY-NINE

she were surveying the room through a kaleidoscope.

Lucy gave her a strange look as if she could see into her soul. She slowly shook her head, no.

"SHUT UP!" she screamed.

Emily's cry choked mid-scream. She hiccupped and looked at Remi with her mouth hanging open. Remi would not be swayed by the illusion of innocence. She needed to lay down the law now, or things would only get worse.

"If you want to scream all the time, we can set up your room in the cellar. How would you like that?"

"Remi!" Mel's shocked voice said from over her shoulder, but Remi chose to ignore it.

"Mama, I scared," Emily hiccupped.

"I don't care," Remi growled. "You are a big girl now. You are too big to be throwing fits. You need your sleep and so does everyone else. I don't want to hear another peep out of you when you're in that bed. Is that understood?"

Before her daughter could answer, Mel roughly grabbed her arm and pulled her from the room before snapping the door shut. "What the hell is wrong with you?"

"What the hell is wrong with me?" Remi laughed maniacally. "What the hell is wrong with me? That's the only question anyone ever seems to ask around here. Maybe the question should be what the hell is wrong with her that she screams her head off every time we put her down?"

"She's two years old!"

"You and I both know this is over the top. How the hell are we supposed to get to the bottom of this if nobody ever sleeps?"

"You need to go to bed right now!" Mel pointed down the hall to her bedroom. "You wouldn't be saying that if you weren't so sleep deprived."

"That's what I'm saying!" Remi threw her hands up in the air. "And that's the way it's going to be until the end of time if that girl does not stop having hissy fits!"

"That girl?"

Remi didn't want to look at the disappointment on her friend's face, so she turned on her heel and walked into the nursery.

She was stopped at the sight of a beautiful Black girl standing in front of the crib. She was about fifteen or sixteen, and she scowled as she stared at Remi.

Remi thought the girl looked familiar for a moment, but she couldn't quite place her. Her first assumption was Richard's sisters. Bailey or Callie. But she knew Callie, and she'd seen a video of Bailey. This girl looked similar. She could almost pass for family.

"Leave the child alone," the girl said and spread her arms, as if blocking Remi's access to the crib.

Before she could ask this girl who she was, she felt a sting in her arm, and everything went dark.

CHAPTER FORTY

Remi

Remi was groggy when voices around woke her up. She glanced around and didn't recognize the walls that surrounded her.

"She's waking up," Natalie's voice spoke, and then her friend was over her, offering a hand to help her sit up.

Remi groaned as her bones screamed in protest. It felt like she'd been in that position forever. "Where are we?" she asked.

"Hotel," Richard sat on the foot of her bed and looked at her with concern in his eyes.

"What happened?"

"You went into a rage," Natalie told her. "Screaming at Emily and threatening to lock her in the cellar. It was very *Margaret*."

Remi squeezed her eyes closed and tried to think. She hadn't done that. Had she? Then a cloudy memory surfaced in her brain. She'd done that. She'd threatened to lock Emily in the cellar.

She raised her hand to her mouth and whispered, "Oh my God."

Richard placed a loving hand over hers. "No one blames

you."

Natalie nodded in agreement. "I touched you while you were out. It was a mixture of sleep deprivation and the house."

Remi's breasts ached violently, and tears filled her eyes as her shirt rubbed against her tender nipples. She suddenly clutched them. "How long have I been asleep?"

Richard and Natalie exchanged a look before he answered her. "We've been taking turns sitting with you for almost three days."

Three days? She'd been asleep for three days? How could that even be possible? It was no wonder she could feel her breasts pulsating as if they were on the verge of exploding.

"No," she clutched her breasts harder as if that would change the reality of the situation. "What about Kylie?"

Richard hung his head. "I got formula."

Remi was livid. He knew how important breast feeding was to her. She'd exclusively breast-fed Emily for the first six months of her life and planned to do the same with Kylie. It was an incredible bonding experience for her and her girls.

She would have been fine giving her baby formula if she were unable to produce milk, but that had never been a problem for her. Now, by giving her formula and allowing Remi to sleep for three days, there was a good chance he'd ruined her milk supply. There was a good chance she'd be completely dried up by now, and if by some miracle she were able to produce milk again, Kylie likely wouldn't take her breast again.

"How could you?" she whispered.

"Remi. Baby, you needed sleep."

"I needed to be a mother to my children more."

"Don't be ridiculous," Natalie said sharply. "You were on the verge of a full-on mental breakdown. You were talking like you were Margaret and Emily was Gloria. Do you not get that? Did you think we'd let the girls near you after that little outburst?"

"I would never hurt my girls!" Remi shot from the bed to get in Natalie's face. But her legs turned rubbery, and she had to lean onto a wall to steady herself.

Natalie shook her head. "Didn't Margaret say the exact same thing about Lucy?"

Her friend's eyes were filled with concern, and she shook her head gently. "The kids are top priority right now."

"So, what are you saying?" Remi looked between Richard and Natalie. "Are you saying you're going to keep me from my own children?

"It won't be forever," Richard held up his hands in a gesture of peace that did nothing to calm her rage.

"That is what you're saying. Listen here," she jabbed a finger into his chest, "I'm not the one that's been violent in that house, and I defended you."

"We're being cautious, babe."

"Don't *babe* me."

"It's only until we can dig up more history and figure things out. Mel's working like a fiend."

"And what if she never figures anything out?"

Richard laughed. "Have you met Mel?"

"You can't keep me in here like a prisoner."

The laugh fell from Richard's face. "Of course, you're not a prisoner. You can go anywhere you want. With someone. And I'm sorry, but you're not stepping foot back in the house until this is all settled."

"*He's signed their death warrant,*" Rebecca's voice thundered in her head. "*Without you there to protect them, they're more vulnerable than ever."*

"They'll die if you keep me away."

"Is that a threat?" he asked her coldly.

"No, you dumbass! I don't know how many times I have to tell you what Rebecca said about one of them being meant to end the curse. The house wants to eliminate them!"

Richard gave her a strange look. "The *house* wants to?"

Remi gritted her teeth. "Rebecca told me—"

"Maybe Rebecca's lying to you!" Richard's outburst caused Remi to step back a moment and glare at him. "It wouldn't be the first time we've been misled by a ghost."

Remi pointed to the door. "You need to go."

"Remi—"

"Now."

He sighed and walked to the door.

Remi turned her gaze to Natalie. "You too."

"What did I do?" Natalie asked in surprise.

"You let him do this," Remi said simply. "I expected better from you. Besides, I need time by myself. To think."

"Okay." Natalie nodded her agreement. "But I'm not leaving. I'll be outside."

Another wave of fury shot through Remi. She was being babysat, and it was an extremely humiliating feeling. But she didn't have any other choice, so she nodded. At least she'd be alone in the room.

When Richard and Natalie exited, Remi chewed her lip and tried to think about what she was supposed to do about this.

* * *

CHAPTER FORTY

Remi spent the rest of the day stewing. She didn't want to talk to Richard or Natalie because she couldn't get over the feeling of betrayal.

There was a knock on her door, and she screamed for them to leave her alone.

"Remi?" The voice belonged to Sophia.

Remi opened the door and allowed her friend to enter.

Sophia wore an expression of concern. "What the hell is going on?"

Remi grabbed her arm and guided her over to the bed. She told her the whole story, and by the time she'd finished she was in tears.

Sophia grasped her hand and gave it a gentle squeeze. "You need a decent meal. Let's go to dinner, and we'll talk over where to go from here."

Remi gratefully agreed and was ready to go in five minutes. Sophia let her pick the restaurant, and a half hour later, they were led to a table in Remi's favorite Mexican restaurant.

The waiter put a basket of chips and salsa on the table and left them with menus. As he turned away, she spotted Dani over his shoulder waiting on another table. The girl gave her a strange look before turning away.

"Great," Remi whispered as she grabbed a chip.

"What?"

She jerked her head toward Dani. "I forgot she works here."

"So what if she does?"

"She's looking at me like I'm crazy."

"Ignore her." Sophia narrowed her eyes at Dani and turned to her menu. "We should talk about what happened though."

Remi sighed. "I don't even remember saying that to Emily. I can't believe I was so heartless. But it's clear I was sleep deprived. I would never do that to my girls. You know that, don't you?"

"Of course I do," Sophia smiled. "You're probably the most giving person I know. I can understand how that statement scared him, though."

"Me too!" Remi reached across the table and grabbed Sophia's wrist, making her jerk. "I don't blame him at all for drugging me to make me sleep. But this is overboard. Taking me to a hotel and not letting me around the girls? Not allowing me to go anywhere alone? I can't wrap my brain around that."

Sophia used her other hand to firmly remove Remi's fingers from her wrist. A red mark was left in its place.

"I'm sorry," Remi apologized and put her head in her hands.

"Don't apologize," Sophia said softly. "I'm okay. More importantly, the girls are okay. But you need to ask yourself a question. I understand you're hurt, but do you truly believe it's overboard to take precautions for the sake of your children?"

"I didn't banish him even though he was the violent one!"

Sophia's eyes flashed. "He hit you?"

Shit. She hadn't meant to say that. She knew he hadn't been in his right mind at the time, and she didn't want anyone thinking less of him.

"Answer me!" Sophia insisted.

"It was a misunderstanding," Remi said under her breath. She concentrated hard on her menu even though she already knew it like the back of her hand.

"There is no such thing as a misunderstanding that excuses hitting your wife."

The waiter came over and took their orders before scurrying away with their menus, and Remi's ability to concentrate on something else.

CHAPTER FORTY

"Remi?" Sophia said shrilly.

"Can we drop it, please?"

"No! Remi, if you need help—"

"Oh my God," Remi snapped. "I don't. It's not like that. Sophia, I love you so much for caring, but I need you to accept it when I tell you to let it go."

"I hate to see you teaching your girls that kind of behavior is okay."

Remi slammed her palm down on the table. The people at the next table jumped, but she ignored them and narrowed her eyes on Sophia. "I am sick and tired of everyone telling me how to raise my kids. Don't you start."

"I'm not trying to tell you how to parent," Sophia said softly, flicking her eyes to the people who were still staring. "I know Emily's at an impressionable age. What if he does something to her, and she doesn't tell you because she thinks it's normal? All I'm saying is it's a slippery slope."

"Richard would never do anything to the girls."

"Did you think he would ever do it to you?"

Remi slammed back in her chair and glared at her friend. Why was everyone trying to give her lessons in parenting recently? Especially someone who didn't even have children? It was irksome.

The fury spread through her body, consuming her in an insistent, burning fire. Remi originally thought she'd feel better getting away from the hotel and getting some sleep, but she was angrier than ever.

She looked away from Sophia to see Dani once again staring at her from across the room. The blistering anger was at a boiling point. Enough of this.

Remi shot from her seat and stomped across the room to

Dani. "What is your problem?"

Dani looked up at her with furrowed eyebrows. "Remi? What are you talking about?"

"Don't patronize me! Why are you staring?"

Dani raised an eyebrow. "I don't know what you're talking about. I didn't even know you were here."

"Don't lie to me!" Remi yelled.

She felt a tug on her shoulder to see Sophia trying to pull her back.

"Are you feeling okay?"

Remi jerked toward Dani but was stopped by Sophia's firm grip. "You think I don't know what's going on over there? Everyone talking about me behind my back? You're over here treating me like some kind of freak!"

"Remi, she's not," Sophia hissed in her ear.

"Is there a problem here?" a sharply dressed man approached them. Remi recognized him from previous visits as the manager.

"Ask your waitress!" she jerked her head toward Dani. "She's been staring at me and being very condescending."

The manager turned to Dani. "Do you know this woman?"

"I do, but I have no idea what she's talking about. I didn't even know she was here."

"Yes, you did! I saw you staring! Staring and judging! Who are you? Who are you to judge me?"

The manager spoke to Sophia. "You two need to leave this establishment. Get her out of here."

"Then call Natalie," Dani told her. "She needs to find out why she's acting so crazy."

That was the last straw. No one was going to call her crazy and get away with it. Especially someone who had no clue

CHAPTER FORTY

what was going on behind the walls of her house.

She wrenched herself from Sophia's grasp and flung herself at Dani. The two of them landed on the nearest table. The table broke, and they slammed to the ground, startling the couple that had been eating there.

Remi grabbed a fistful of Dani's hair and slammed her head against the ground once before she was roughly grabbed around the middle and jerked off Dani. She was slammed up against the wall, and her arms were jerked behind her back.

Finally, she registered the flashing red and blue lights shining through the windows of the restaurant.

CHAPTER FORTY-ONE

Margaret

As the years passed, Margaret felt darker by the day. Everything enraged her. With each owner that entered the house, she'd get more and more annoyed. It would be abundantly clear each time they wouldn't be the ones to help her girls, so she'd chase them away.

Every time she chased them off, something else would happen to her soul. Her horns grew longer, her skin bluer, she developed scales over every inch of her body. And she reveled in it.

The others would all whisper behind their hands and flee from the room when she entered. As if she were something on the bottom of their shoes. Luckily, she was long past the point of caring.

Something about meeting Sadie unlocked a part of her that was buried deep within. She didn't quite understand it, but now she could show herself at will to anyone she pleased and could move objects. That's why it never made any sense to her why the others judged her for it. They could all do it, they all had at some point. But when she did it, somehow, it was

CHAPTER FORTY-ONE

the most awful thing imaginable.

Maybe it was because she willfully disregarded the rules, but that was her right. She was the mistress of Blackwood Manor. She had been for many years. Who were they to tell her what she could and could not do in her own house? Who she could and could not talk to?

If anyone stayed in the house, it would be because she allowed it, and so far she hadn't found anyone worthy of the privilege. One day, Josie told her that people were scared of the property and didn't want to come near it. Good. That's the way she wanted it. Then one night, there was a noticeable shift in the dynamic.

She was pacing in the attic when she was overcome with a strange feeling. She felt—power. It wasn't clear at first where it came from, but the property seemed to radiate with it. Then she heard it. The sound of a window breaking. She used her energy to make herself invisible and traveled to the room the noise came from. The front parlor.

Margaret watched with seething anger as a group of four teenagers crawled through the window. Not only did they have the audacity to break the window and come into *her* house, but they weren't even a respectful group of kids.

They wore garish costumes that mocked the sorry state she was currently forced to live in. One annoying boy in a black and white striped suit with ridiculous makeup grabbed a pretty black girl wearing a nurse outfit and tilted her backward to kiss her. Her short dress rode up, and Margaret was disgusted to see that she wasn't wearing underwear.

The boy groped her breast, and the two other kids stood to the side and exchanged awkward glances.

The suit boy looked at the other one and winked. "Happy

Halloween, ehh, Dono?"

What kind of name was Dono?

"Happy Halloween," Dono chuckled. Margaret felt nervousness running off him. Maybe that one wasn't so bad. The others, though, were already working on her nerves. She had a feeling she was going to have to work in overdrive to scare this group off. The property nearly vibrated with the force of the power that came with this group, but she wasn't sure which of them was causing it. Surely these weren't the ones destined to help her girls? They were awful.

The nurse grabbed the suit boy's hand and led him seductively toward the doorway. "Well, we'll leave you two alone to get—acquainted."

The one called Dono smiled awkwardly when they were alone. "So."

"So," the girl said and pulled down the skirt of her green dress.

"We don't have to do anything."

"Good. Because I'm not that kind of girl."

"Alright." He gestured for them to sit on the ground.

"So," she said again, "military, huh? I bet you've seen lots of cool stuff."

He shrugged. "Not really. I've lived in a lot of places, but we never stay anywhere for long. It's usually just school and home. That's pretty much the same everywhere."

"No extracurriculars?"

Even in the dark Margaret could see him blush. "No. It's not that I'm not interested in anything. It's that there's no point in getting involved. I don't want to commit to something I can't finish."

"That's actually pretty noble."

CHAPTER FORTY-ONE

"You think?"

"Yeah. Totally. Most guys I know only care about the glory. For as long as it lasts. They don't care about how many people they screw over when they don't follow through."

"So, what extracurriculars are you into?"

"You'll think I'm a dork."

He tilted his head to the side. "Do I look like someone who cares about that?"

She laughed. "I'm on yearbook."

"You're kidding? That's rad."

"You think so?"

"Yeah. You're conserving memories for the entire school. Forever immortalizing them. That's very rad."

Margaret didn't know what "rad" was, but it sounded like a compliment. This yearbook thing sounded incredible. Immortalizing everyone? She wished she had a yearbook of her own. Maybe if she did, she wouldn't feel like the shell she currently was. What she wouldn't give to be able to live on forever. These two weren't so bad. They were definitely better than the other two. She hoped one of them was the powerful one.

"I wish everyone was like you," the girl blushed and looked down at her lap. "I mean that most people aren't that accepting. If you're not a jock or cheerleader, you're not anyone."

"Ty and Donna like you."

She shook her head. "Ty tolerates me. Donna and I grew up on the same block and became friends when we were seven. Sometimes I think she only hangs out with me now out of loyalty, not because she actually likes me."

Margaret felt a twinge in her chest. She understood that feeling. She'd felt that way about Josie the last few years before her death.

"I'm sure that's not true. Every time I hang out with her and Ty, she talks about you all the time."

"Well, that's because she wants me to have a boyfriend. So we can double. She's tired of me being the third wheel." The girl threw a glance over her shoulder before she turned back to him. "Want to know a secret?"

He leaned in closer and nodded his head.

"I'm not so sure I like her either."

"Really?"

She nodded. "She's kind of gotten snobby. It's all about her and her lifestyle. She doesn't want anything to do with anything that can put a cramp in it. Like leaving her sister out there?" She jerked her head toward the window. "It bugs me. I'm an only child, right? My parents almost didn't have me. I always dreamed of having a sister. Seeing the way she treats Emma really gets under my skin. It's like she's an annoying pest that needs to be squashed. Her parents told her she needed to take her trick or treating. She didn't take that poor girl to one house. Just brought her here and left her in the car."

"I figured they went already."

"No. She'd have to actually do something."

Margaret's fury built again, and she glanced up to the floor above. That girl left her sister locked in something called a car while she went upstairs to have relations with a boy? In *Margaret's* house? Well, she'd see about that.

* * *

CHAPTER FORTY-ONE

When Margaret found the teens, they were half naked in *her* bed. Enough of this. She let her defenses down to allow herself to be seen. She hovered over the bed for a moment and waited.

The girl opened her eyes and screamed. "Ty! Ty! Behind you!"

Margaret swiped a claw out and knocked the boy across the room. He crumpled to the ground, and she made herself invisible again.

The girl rushed across the room to him, hurriedly trying to button her nurse top. "Ty?" she whispered.

Margaret felt the crippling pain that was so familiar, and her mind became a dark blur.

CHAPTER FORTY-TWO

Remi

Remi sat up when the door to the interrogation room opened. She'd lost track of how much time she'd sat in that room with her forehead resting on the cold, metal table in front of her.

The sheriff came in with a tall, skinny man in a suit. she'd never seen before. The man carried a briefcase and wore a smug expression.

"Mrs. Price?"

She nodded at the man.

"I'm Jared Russell. Your husband retained me as your counsel."

Remi looked at the sheriff nervously and the lawyer followed her gaze.

"The sheriff here is going to give us a few minutes alone to talk."

The sheriff nodded in agreement. "I just wanted to check if you need anything first."

Remi shook her head and wiped her sweaty hands on her jeans as she watched the two men exchange a few words. This

CHAPTER FORTY-TWO

was serious. She didn't know what she'd been thinking at the restaurant, but she knew she was in a world of trouble now.

The door to the interrogation room closed again and the lawyer sat across from her. He didn't smile or give her any other sign of encouragement. She had no clue how bad it was going to be for her.

"You've had an eventful week, haven't you?"

Week? This wasn't about the restaurant? What all was he referring to?

"Do you understand what we're dealing with?" he prompted.

"How bad is it?"

"Well, they're holding you for destruction of public property and aggravated assault."

She couldn't help the condescending laugh. "I think that's a bit of an exaggeration."

"You tackled a waitress into a customer's table, grabbed a fistful of hair, and slammed her head into the ground, and broke her nose."

"She should have answered my question."

Russell put a pen down in front of him on the table. "You have to work with me here, Remi. So far, you don't have a defense. There are dozens of witnesses who saw you attack that girl unprovoked. You can't deny it. Honestly, this behavior is giving more weight to the report that was placed about possible abuse in the home. Child protective service may reopen the case."

"No, no. They can't do that," Remi sat forward and pleaded with him. "That had nothing to do with what happened at the restaurant."

"Maybe not. But it calls into question your behavior when you're upset."

Shit. Shit. Shit. It wasn't supposed to be like this. That issue was supposed to be over and done with. There's no way they would believe the truth.

"Do you want to tell me what happened?"

"What did they tell you happened?"

He sighed. "You don't make things easy, do you?" He tapped the pen on the table again before finally telling her. "Your husband and friend that was with you, Sophia, both say you'd convinced yourself that he was sleeping with the waitress."

Remi's skin crawled at that explanation, but she understood. They had to say something, and an affair was really the only reason that could logically explain her attacking Dani.

"But I don't believe that," he told her.

"Oh, you don't?"

He shook his head. "Because you see, pretty much the entire restaurant staff said that those claims are ridiculous. It's well known that Danielle Larson is a lesbian. She happens to be in a long-term relationship with Natalie Morgan."

"Huh. Interesting."

"Natalie Morgan works at your bed & breakfast, doesn't she?"

"She does."

"So, is there any truth to their claims?"

"Well, if they said it, it must be true."

"Okay, Remi," he sighed again and rose from his seat to knock on the door to the interrogation room. "I guess we can bring the sheriff back in."

* * *

CHAPTER FORTY-TWO

When Remi was led to a cell an hour later, she was shaking. She hadn't expected to spend the night in jail. She'd broken some dishes at the restaurant. She figured she'd get a fine…maybe community service. She didn't know she'd broken Dani's nose. Of course, that would make her look like a violent psychopath.

"Well, well, look what the cat dragged in," her father pressed his smug face up against the bars of the cell opposite hers. "I knew they'd eventually come to their senses."

Remi rolled her eyes. With everything that recently happened, she forgot her father was still here. "I got into a fight. It'll be sorted out by morning. It had nothing to do with my kids, you psychotic bastard. But your phony CPS case might get reopened."

He laughed. "I never called child protective services, but I wish I did. You and your husband both acted like a couple of loonies the whole time we were there. You should be locked away and those girls sent to a more stable, loving home."

Remi sneered at him. "Like the one I grew up in?"

"You grew up like a princess. You were given every opportunity for a good life. It's not our fault if you fucked it up and threw it all away."

"I have a successful business and am going to be a doctor. I'd hardly call that throwing it all away."

He scoffed. "You run a glorified motel. The only reason it gets any business at all is a torrid history."

Remi tried to keep her expression neutral, but couldn't stop the blush from heating her cheeks. So, he did know about the house's history. She didn't know if she should be surprised or not.

He sneered at her. "Yes, I know your dirty little secret. Honestly, what you're doing is exploitative. You're cashing in on other's misfortune and pain."

"You're crazy," she hissed. "They should lock you up and throw away the key." She laid down on the thin mattress of her cot and rolled the opposite way.

He chuckled. "We'll see who's laughing in the end."

Before she drifted off to sleep, Remi couldn't stop thinking about her father's words. Were they exploitative for running the bed & breakfast? Or were they merely restoring a magnificent building to its former beauty?

CHAPTER FORTY-THREE

Remi

"Price! Price! Get up!"

Remi was awoken by sharp banging on the bars right above her head, making her jump. She sat up and looked at the sour-faced officer who made the offending noise.

"You made bail. Let's go."

She rose to her feet and bit down the pain that spread through her muscles. She walked out the door as he swung it open, and waited for a jeering remark from her father, who she didn't bother to look at. Luckily, he kept his jabs to himself for once in his life. She was much too tired to deal with his antics today.

As the officer led Remi from the holding cells and to the front lobby, it occurred to her that she hadn't had any Margaret memory dreams while she'd been locked up. Somehow, it did nothing to ease her mind. The realization sent a cold shiver down her spine, as if catastrophe was waiting around the corner.

She was led through a doorway and out to a desk where her

personal belongings were returned to her. She was dismissed at that point and walked out to chairs where Richard was waiting for her. He didn't say anything when they walked to the car, or when they started driving toward the house.

"We're not going back to the motel?" she asked him with a shaky voice.

"What's the point?" His tone was clipped. "Apparently, it didn't help your bizarre behavior. We might as well save money and keep you at home where we can keep an eye on you."

His words stung, but she couldn't argue with his logic. She'd behaved horribly. Worst of all, the behavior was aimed at someone she liked and respected. She'd replayed the events in her mind over and over while she waited in the jail cell. No matter how hard she tried, she couldn't figure out what she'd been thinking.

She swallowed back a lump in her throat for the first time as she imagined what Natalie's reaction would be when she saw her. It could honestly go either way.

Remi held her breath when Richard pulled into the driveway and parked in their small parking area. He didn't speak to her or wait. He got out of the car and walked up to the door with her trailing several feet behind.

She'd no more than walked in the door when Natalie grasped her arm, startling her. She braced herself to be struck, but the blow didn't come.

Natalie released her arm and stepped back. There was no anger on her face. The only thing resting in her features was concern.

Remi looked at her friend regretfully. "I don't know what I was thinking."

CHAPTER FORTY-THREE

"Let's sit down," Natalie gestured for the parlor, and they walked in to sit on the couches. Remi threw a look back into the foyer.

"Who's manning the desk?"

"We don't have any guests," Richard said from where he leaned against the doorframe.

Remi felt instant shame even though she knew the lack of guests was not her fault. They'd been booked solid for months. Now they were back to no guests. Just like the good old days.

One by one, Mel, Gus, Deacon, and Jessie joined them in the parlor.

"Where's Sophia?" Remi asked.

They all exchanged glances before Natalie spoke up. "She didn't show up today. She was very upset when she called Richard last night. About a lot of things."

"She went along with my cover story for the police, but she said she was done beyond that. It's too much drama for her."

Remi's heart sank. She never would have expected Sophia to turn on her. But she'd witnessed Remi acting like a mad woman over nothing. Remi couldn't even imagine how that must have looked to someone on the outside looking in.

"We have a lot to talk about," Natalie went on. "Mel's been working like crazy the last few days to find anything that could help us."

Mel slid some photos across the table for Remi to look at. "Let's go back to the symbols on the wall. We were looking at them wrong at first. They aren't phrases. They're just words. Hundreds of them. But they all seem to allude to the same thing."

Remi looked at the photographs. They weren't the same pictures she'd taken with her phone the morning after the

Henderson's left. These were photos from a similar scene with reference translations spelled out. "Die. Cry. Sorrow. Misery." Then there was the one that gave Remi the ultimate chill. "Mind-control."

She repeated it in a whisper and ran her fingertips along the photo in question.

"That's what we think is happening," Mel took it and gave her hand a gentle squeeze. Remi's heart thunked with an unnatural rhythm. She felt as if she'd been given a death sentence, but Mel wore a smile on her face.

"Why are you smiling?" Remi asked.

"Because we're a step ahead for once. I found a case very similar to this one that happened in Massachusetts. A woman started behaving strangely following disturbed sleep. At one point, she was acting exactly like a notorious resident of the home."

"She was possessed." Remi didn't understand why they were acting like this was such a big revelation. Possession was nothing new to this group.

"No. Not possessed," Mel protested. "They knew for a fact that spirit was not in the home anymore."

"Then what?"

Natalie scooted closer. "You're experiencing an imprint. Basically, Margaret's gone, but her memories imprinted in the house and have latched on to you. That's why you dream about her thoughts and actions."

"Why do you all seem so excited? This is terrifying."

"Don't you see?" Natalie asked impatiently. "If we can put Margaret at peace, then your dreams will stop. We can neutralize them."

Remi looked around at her friends. While she appreciated

CHAPTER FORTY-THREE

their dedication and optimism, she didn't agree with the logic. She was the one in Margaret's head, after all. And two things made Remi believe she'd never get out of this. One was that Margaret's spirit was gone. How could they put a spirit to rest that no longer existed? The second was the things she saw while she was in Margaret's head. Something made Margaret do the things she did. If Margaret was in Remi's head, who was in Margaret's?

Remi smiled at her friends and slowly rose to her feet. "Can we talk about this later, guys? I'm really tired. The bed at the jail wasn't too comfortable."

They all told her to get rest and let her walk away.

She was nearly to the staircase when she caught a whispered phrase. *"Should we tell her what that officer said?"*

She bit down the anger as she stomped up the stairs. They were still talking about her behind her back. It wasn't that she cared what the stupid police officer said about her, but they should have told her what it was regardless. It was the principle of it. If someone says something nasty about someone close to you, you tell them. What kind of friend are you, otherwise?

CHAPTER FORTY-FOUR

Margaret

Margaret didn't know what happened. The next thing she knew, she was standing on the grounds out back. The boy from the parlor, Dono, was wrestling on the ground with a dirty, greasy man to gain control of a large butcher knife. Who was this man? Where did he come from? A pretty, Black girl sat on the ground a few feet away. She cried hysterically. She wasn't much older than her Lucy, eight at the most.

Margaret could help. She nearly did. Then she felt the heat radiating off the young girl. It was a very clear, underdeveloped sense of power, and it scared Margaret. It stopped her in her tracks. Suddenly, she knew. *She can help my girls.* It wasn't Dono at all. It was her. This little girl.

A cold voice hissed over her shoulder. "To do that, she'll have to end you. Is that what you want? To be obliterated as if you never mattered at all?"

Margaret didn't even think. She rushed forward. Dono's eyes met hers over the shoulder of his assailant. He jerked his eyes over to the little girl.

CHAPTER FORTY-FOUR

"EMMA! RUN!"

Margaret grabbed the greasy man's hand, let out an otherworldly howl, and shoved the knife into Dono's sternum all the way up to the hilt. She then tossed the man to the side like a sack of potatoes. Then she looked for the girl.

Margaret roamed the grounds with a purpose. She hadn't noticed the girl running away, but then, she'd been preoccupied. She grew steadily angrier as each location she checked gave her no answers.

When she reached the strange carriage that the group arrived in, she wrenched open the metal door and tossed aside blankets in her search for the girl.

Then she heard a loud screech from the road a few feet away. When she looked up, another carriage stopped on the road, with strange lights casting a glow on everything in front of it. The girl stood in the road waving her hands.

The person in the carriage threw open their door and ran toward her. Then they looked toward the house, with eyes full of horror. The adult scooped her up in their arms and ran back to their carriage.

Margaret growled and raced toward them, but a force stopped her and threw her back. She couldn't go past the property line. How was she supposed to eliminate the threat if she couldn't go past the property line?

She let out another almighty howl as the carriage sped away with the girl inside.

"She'll be back," a sing-song voice mocked her from nearby. "And when she does, you better be ready."

Margaret was in a fog as she walked back to the house. Most of the night was a blur. She'd found the group of teenagers annoying and wanted to scare them away. She'd definitely wanted to dispose of the small girl. The power that radiated off her was terrifying.

When she forced herself to go into the house, she was prepared. The spirits of the newly dead teenagers were hysterical. New death was often like that. Margaret almost preferred it when they didn't realize they were dead right away. It was much less stressful.

The boy in the striped suit lay in almost the exact same place Josie did when she'd died. His spirit stood over the body with wide eyes and his jaw hanging open.

The girl in the nurse uniform stood in the parlor staring at her body. Her hands were clasped against each cheek, and she screamed at the top of her lungs. That was going to be a fun one.

The girl in the short green dress glided down the stairs with a glazed expression on her face. "I'm dead," she said in a strange monotone.

"News flash," the boy said sharply before looking at her. "We're all dead."

Dono walked into the entryway. He gave her a hard stare as the knife wounds in his chest and stomach disappeared before her eyes.

Margaret was bewildered. She'd never seen wounds that were there at the time of death disappear before. Josie didn't have a face because it was obliterated in her fall, Lucy still had the bullet wound in her chest. How was this boy who'd died only minutes before able to heal his wounds?

"Guys. Guys!" he yelled over his friend's screaming, silencing them. "We gotta talk."

CHAPTER FORTY-FIVE

Remi

Remi decided to stop by and talk to Emily before retiring to her room. She felt horrible about what she'd said the other night and needed to make it right with her daughter.

But when she walked in the bedroom Emily wasn't there. "Emily!" she called out and checked the closet before concluding she wasn't in the room at all.

Remi went straight to the nursery and saw Emily wasn't in there either. She turned toward the door to go check the bathroom when she was struck by a strange feeling. She walked to the crib in three long strides and looked into it. Kylie did not lie inside. She knew the girls hadn't been downstairs. Where were the girls?

"Richard! RICHARD!" she screamed and flew around the room to search in every nook and cranny.

Footsteps thundered in the hall, and she twirled toward the door with panicked eyes. "The girls are gone! Someone took the girls!"

"Honey!" he grabbed her firmly but gently by the shoulders

and looked deep into her eyes. "No one took them."

"They didn't?"

He shook his head. "No. The way you've been acting lately has scared me. It's scared everyone. I made arrangements for them to go someplace safe."

She was horrified. "You gave our girls away?"

"No! Nothing like that. It's temporary. Just until we find a way to end whatever it is that's making you act like this."

Remi slapped his hands away. "That's forever! This place has had evil in it for hundreds of years! Do you really think you're going to banish it in a couple of days or weeks? Where are they?"

He took a deep breath, dropped his hands from her arms and looked at her with tear-filled eyes. "I'm sorry. I can't tell you that."

"You bastard!" she screeched and lunged forward to beat at his chest with her fists. He didn't try to fight back, only placed his forearms in front of him to take the brunt of the blows. "Tell me where they are, you son of a bitch!" She swiped at him with her nails.

"Remi! Calm down!" Natalie grabbed her from behind and attempted to pin her arms to her side. Remi threw her weight back to try and knock the other woman off balance.

Finally, her energy was spent, and she crumpled to the floor, sobbing. Everyone she knew betrayed her. It was beyond devastating.

"It's not forever, Remi," Natalie whispered in her ear. "It's for their safety. You'll thank us later."

Would she? Remi felt that was debatable.

Richard knelt in front of her. "Honey?" he asked cautiously. "Please tell me you understand. We always said we'd do what

CHAPTER FORTY-FIVE

was best for them. No matter how hard it was."

She continued to look at the ground. They said that. It didn't make the reality of the situation any easier to tolerate.

"Remi?"

Epilogue

Mel

Mel sighed when her phone screen lit up. Her sister Cindy had been calling her nonstop, and she wasn't ready to deal with her. She couldn't put it off anymore.

She took a deep breath and answered. "Yeah?"

"Where are you? I thought you'd be back by now?" Her sister's shrill voice tore through the silence.

"I'm still at Blackwood Manor. Things are bad."

"Well, things are bad here too, and I would think your family would come first!"

That was an interesting mentality to have after everything Cindy did, but Mel knew better than to bring that up right now. "What's so bad?"

"The staff are being attacked. What are we going to do?"

Mel sighed. She'd been afraid of this, but hoped the time wouldn't come so soon. Hotel Dahlia changed dramatically since she'd grown up there. She was sad to see the changes when she went home. "Okay. Give me a couple of days to make arrangements. I'll be there as soon as I can."

EPILOGUE

"Bring that psychic you told me about."

"Why?"

"You said yourself that we haven't been able to get help from anyone credible. You said this girl knows her stuff."

"She does."

"So, bring her."

Mel didn't have a chance to respond before Cindy hung up. She growled and stomped into the kitchen where the others were having breakfast.

Remi sat in a chair with her arms crossed over her chest. She'd barely spoken to anyone since she'd come home from jail to find that her two daughters were relocated. Poor thing. Remi was a good person. When she had a chance to realize everything they were doing for her she'd be grateful. Until then, she'd be in pain. Mel wished there was another way.

"Hey, what's wrong with you?" Natalie asked.

"Cindy called. The staff is being attacked. I have to go."

"What?" Richard asked in alarm as he looked up from his pancakes.

"That's not the worst of it," Mel pressed on. "She wants me to bring you."

Richard shot to his feet. "What? No. You can't leave. Either one of you. We need you here."

Richard jerked his head in Remi's direction, and Mel nodded slightly. She understood what he was getting at. The woman had become unpredictable, and he didn't want to be alone with her. She wouldn't want to be either.

"Relax, Richard." Natalie held up a hand to calm him down. "How urgent is this?"

"I'm guessing bad. She was near hysterical on the phone. The juju was bad before I left. All the psychics we brought in were crackpots."

Natalie tsked. "They make a bad name for all of us."

"You're not actually considering this?" Richard asked.

"It's okay," Natalie smiled and turned her gaze back to Mel. "We'll all go. We can multi-task, right?"

"I think so," Mel nodded in agreement.

Natalie turned to Remi and smiled. "What do you think, Remi? Ever been to New Orleans?"

Remi rolled her eyes and didn't answer.

"Will that really work?" Richard asked.

Natalie shrugged. "I don't see why not. We don't have any guests right now."

Mel shot Richard a regretful smile. The business was rapidly sliding down the tubes. She hoped they'd be able to turn things around before their reputation was too badly trashed.

"Okay," Richard agreed, but Mel could see the nerves on his face.

"Alright, I'll call the airline to get tickets," Natalie said.

Mel's emotions were mixed. She was glad to turn some focus back to Hotel Dahlia, but she couldn't help but eye Remi, who stared at the wall with a blank face. Mel's gut told her that woman was going to be a problem.

Thank you so much for reading! I hope you enjoyed this continuation into the Blackwood Manor universe.

About the Author

Hi there! I'm Ashley Bundy and I'm so happy you picked up my little book baby. I enjoy a good spellbinding mystery, so I thought it would be a good idea if I wrote a few! I like to weave fictional stories with my real-life experiences to make them feel more raw.

The Blackwood Manor duology is based on a couple of haunted houses from my childhood. One was my childhood home, and one was my best friend's. Between the two of us the houses told endless stories. Some of our actual experiences are in these two books, but I'm not saying which ones. You'll just have to guess!! Happy reading!

Dreams of Darkness is a continuation of that lovely saga. I had so much more story to tell, and I couldn't ruin it for you lovely readers, could I?

You can connect with me on:
- https://ashleybundy.wixsite.com/my-site-1
- https://x.com/bookloverbundy2
- https://facebook.com/ashleybundyauthor
- https://facebook.com/ashley%E2%80%99sbookbungalow
- https://www.instagram.com/ashleybundyreads
- https://www.tiktok.com/@ashleybundybooks
- https://www.goodreads.com/goodreadscomashley_bundy
- https://www.bookbub.com/profile/ashley-bundy

Also by Ashley Bundy

The Blackwood Manor Duology
Blackwood Manor
The Haven Stone

Standalones
Disappearance on Route 6

www.ingramcontent.com/pod-product-compliance
Lightning Source LLC
LaVergne TN
LVHW091633070526
838199LV00044B/1042